TO HELL WITH THAT JOB

A GUIDE TO LIVING YOUR DREAMS

Yuvaan
books
An Imprint of Unbound Script

To Hell With That Job

Written *by* Vijeta Dahiya

First Edition : January, 2026

ISBN : 978-93-47125-08-9

Publisher : Unbound Script
2/41, Ansari Road
Daryaganj, Delhi-110002
Website : www.unboundscript.com
E-mail : books@unboundscript.com
Phone : 011-35807601

Printer : Yash Printographics
Noida, Uttar Pradesh

Price : ₹ 399/-

TO HELL WITH THAT JOB

A GUIDE TO LIVING YOUR DREAMS

VIJETA DAHIYA

Yuvaan
books

CONTENTS

Chapter -1

The Unique Fantasies

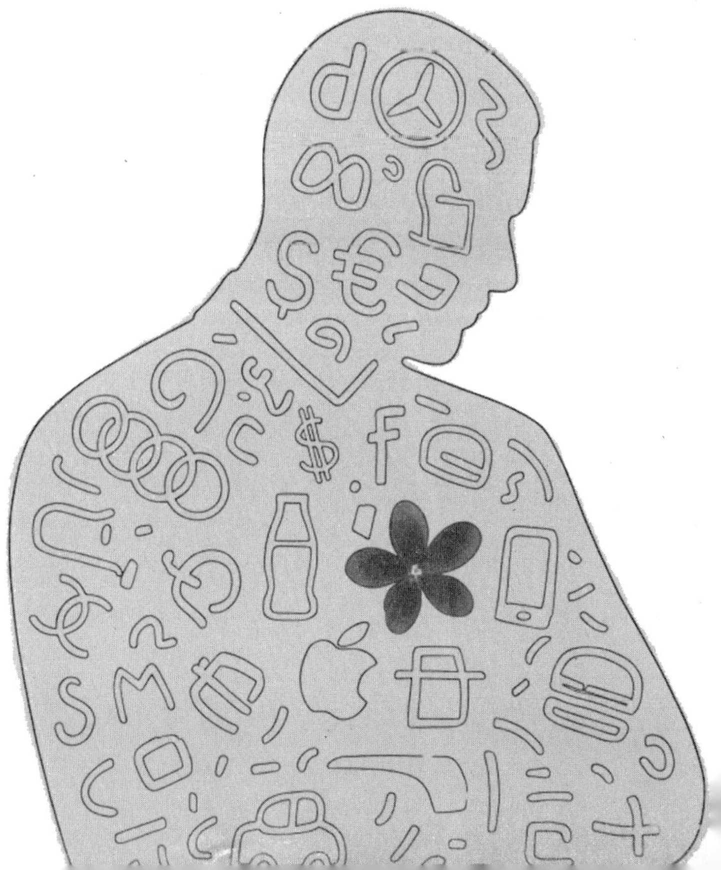

My girlfriend said, "Let's go and watch the next FIFA World Cup live."

I said, "Hmm!"

"Hmm, what? Will we go or not? Promise that you'll take me."

If I ask her to name three football teams, I bet she won't know even one! But since everyone in the corporate world is watching the Football World Cup, she wants to do the same.

"What a copycat she is!" That's what I thought, but I didn't say it.

Instead, I said: "What's the big deal about watching it live? It looks great on TV– you can see everything up close. In the big stadium, you can hardly see the tiny ball properly, or even any player's faces clearly. Watching it on TV is watching it live too. Plus, you get replays here."

"There are huge screens in the stadium as well for watching the replays."

"But we're already watching it on a screen, comfortably in our own space. We're eating snacks. Want some coffee?"

"Oh! Come on! It's a whole different vibe, going there and experiencing it in person. It's a different experience! Plus, we'll get to travel to another country. So stop making silly excuses. Promise me that we'll go."

Now what do I say? Saying a straight 'no' doesn't feel right. So I try to dodge with some excuses. But she's not getting it. Eventually, I just blurt it out -

"I'm not going to make such a promise. Sorry."

She looked at me, surprised. "What's your problem?"

"You know I might quit my job anytime, right?"

"Yeah, so what?"

Is she not getting this simple point? I began to explain in detail, "Look, to go to another country, you need to take a flight. You need to book hotels. For all that, you need money. Money comes from salary. Salary comes from working. If I quit my job, I won't have money. Get it?"

"You're not going to just sit idle after quitting your job. You'll pursue your dreams– write books, make films, and even act, maybe. Money is not going to be an issue."

Classic technique! Just butter someone up and then ask for whatever you want. But I'm not one to fall for that.

"Yeah, the whole world is just waiting for me to quit my job, make a little effort, and then the offers will start pouring in. Shahrukh Khan himself is going to beg me - 'Vijeta ji, please act in my film!'"

She looked at me, annoyed. Stayed quiet for five seconds. Then sighed deeply and said, "So you think you won't get work? You've given up before even trying? If you don't have hope, then what's the point of trying? You should have faith in your dreams, in your talent. Really, you should be the one offering to take me to the next FIFA World Cup."

"I do have hope and faith - that's precisely why I'm thinking of quitting my job. But nothing is 100% certain! All I can do is play my part, which I will. But who knows whether things will work out or not- there are seventy other factors involved. Who knows, maybe four years from now, things won't have changed much. Maybe we won't have enough money- "

"There you go again. Why wouldn't you? Be positive!"

"I am being positive. Don't you get it? Nothing is ever 100% sure. There's always some risk involved."

We're talking about my dreams, but the way she looked at me, it felt like I'd crushed hers instead. Maybe I did. A few days ago, we were watching a movie with scenes of the Pyramids of Egypt, and she said, "We will also go to the pyramids, won't we?".

"Yeah, sure, we will go," I replied.

Well, obviously this means that the responsibility of earning for these trips falls on me. Otherwise her legs work just fine too - it's not like I have to carry her in my lap everywhere!

Well, she can demand even that. She can expect anything from me. But why, though? The right to expect anything from me used to belong only to my father. To see dreams on my behalf and then to impose them upon me. He wanted me to become an IAS officer. Now he wants me to travel to America at the company's expense so that he can blow his trumpet at the park in the evening.

My name was on the list for a work visit to the US office. I told this at home. It was going to be a one-week visit. Beyond my dad's dreams for me, my own personal self was pretty pleased too– thinking about getting to see America and all. But something changed between Friday and Monday. Some storm blew in; my dad's trumpet got shattered. The opportunity slipped out of my hands and went to my co-worker instead. So what? Let it go.

I thought that if I became a film star, I'd make the producer shoot a song in America. Maybe one in front of the pyramids too. That would keep this copycat happy– she could post photos on Facebook. And what if that didn't work out? What if I didn't get film roles? And after a break in my corporate career, it's tough to get another job. And then? Long live my dream of opening a tea stall!

I once had tea at a shop in Dehradun. The first thing I noticed: it was so clean. There were tables and benches to sit on. No flies buzzing around. It wasn't dark or dingy inside. There was a door at the back opening into the courtyard of the owner's house. Second, the boy served tea in a glass, not in one of those disposable paper cups with plastic lining that leaches microplastics into your tea. The glass was properly washed. Third, along with tea, there were options for rusks, crispy fan puffs, biscuits, and even omelette.

And above all, the tea was truly outstanding! Some tea vendors add too much water; some don't boil it enough. If you ask for sugarless tea, they'll make it from already-used tea leaves– and then it tastes sweet even without adding sugar. Some don't bother adding ginger or cardamom. I tell them, "Charge me 25 instead of 15, but give me a refreshing cup of tea." Still, good tea is a rarity. I've almost stopped having tea outside now– except at Chaayos. They serve good tea in clay cups, but at 150 bucks a cup. But here, this boy gave amazing tea for just 15 rupees. I had another cup; so did my friends.

Delhi could really use a tea shop like that. If I open such a shop, will I always enjoy making tea? When customers take a sip and find joy, will the contentment on their faces make my life feel meaningful? Yes, it would. To think that I've satisfied the souls of thousands of tea lovers– life would feel worthwhile. But then, won't I get bored making tea every day?

Sunil sir wasn't wrong. Actually, his name isn't Sunil, but for the sake of the book, I've changed everyone's names– so let's stick with Sunil. He had started four companies and divested each one as soon as it took off. I once told him, "Sir, the hardest part is starting a business. Later on, it's all about sitting back and reaping the rewards. And you sell your businesses just when they pick up, only to start a new one and take that headache all over again."

He said, "Vijeta, I don't enjoy running a business; I enjoy starting one. The stuff you call a headache– that's what's fun for me. Coming up with a new business idea, designing the product or service, standardising operations, streamlining processes, marketing– turning an idea into a real business before my eyes. That's what I find challenging, and that's what I enjoy the most."

I would really enjoy opening a tea shop like this– a neat little place where you get amazing tea served in glass cups, along with a few snack options. But my idea goes way beyond that. There would be chess for people to play. Of course, there would be a separate charge– but only the winner would pay. It wouldn't be fair to charge the loser– one who's already upset about losing.

If you want, you could just sit there and read a novel. Or maybe write a story or a poem. If you want to show off your poetry or paintings, there would be a bulletin board– you could pin up your work, and others could leave comments. Kind of like an offline Instagram. If anyone wants to put up an advertisement or a business poster, there would be a charge for that.

Once a week, there would be some kind of event– like a discussion on neighbourhood issues every Friday evening at 6 pm. If you have a petition for your local councillor, MLA, or MP, you could post it on the bulletin board for free and others could sign. I've heard that in Kolkata, there used to be tea shops where intellectuals would gather to talk about literature, music, cinema, and society. Maybe once in a while, we'll have something like that– with a moderator, a discussion over tea.

Eventually, I would open multiple branches– maybe even offer franchises, but only on the condition that neither the quality nor the overall model is compromised. One day, I would sell it off for crores, just like Sunil sir did. Once my dream of creating this tea shop is fulfilled, someone else could take over. With all that money, I'll go and make a movie. No, I won't put all the money into the film. I'll keep most of it in my account, maybe invest a little, and use only part of it for the movie. But what if the film flops? What if it doesn't make any money?

Well, then I can always teach kids. Back in college, I used to tutor children from second grade all the way to first-year college. But I won't open a tuition centre– I'll start my own school. Each class would have 25 students. That would make around 300 students from grades 1 to 12. Only twelve classrooms. No mindless rote learning. Whether it's maths or science, everything would be taught conceptually, through hands-on experience.

From the very first grade, children would learn reasoning and psychology, so they become rational human beings– who know how to control their ego, greed, anger, jealousy, and hatred. From childhood, they would be involved in calisthenics; play football, basketball, and badminton; learn classical music properly; paint; do theatre; read great literature; write stories and poems; and watch world cinema.

There would be a field in the school, where kids could grow vegetables and crops. They would get business training too. Sometimes, they would go on trips to a bird sanctuary, other times to a science exhibition. This way, by the time they reach tenth grade, they would know about every career; they would have a little exposure to every field. These kids would be the country's future leaders. They would win the Nobel Prize in chemistry, bring home Olympic medals, and start international theatre companies.

And then I would set up such schools in every district of the country. That's going to cost a lot. So would only rich kids get to study there, the ones who can pay hefty monthly fees? No way. I'll have to figure something out. Maybe 12 out of every 25 kids will be from millionaire families, paying lakhs in fees, and the remaining 13 could be anyone– they would attend the school for free. Or maybe I'll ask Dhruv to collect donations for the school from everyone in the country, so all children can study for free.

And then I'll make the kind of movie I want. The very first dream is to be an artist. If that doesn't work out, then the next dream follows. Like the tea shop is one dream, and this unique school is another. Can someone really have so many dreams? Why not!

Well, opening a school like this is as tough as becoming an artist, but a tea shop– yeah, I could manage that. But would that feel like a compromise? Not to me. I'll do theatre on the side and write a little, too.

But the world would just say, "He couldn't make it as a big artist, so he opened a tea shop." If there are 100 branches of my tea shop, then everyone will shower praise. They would heap accolades on me. But if it's just one shop and I'm the one actually making the tea, they'll say, "What a fool! He left a great job chasing his artist dream, and look, now he's selling tea."

What's the difference between one shop and a hundred? A whole lot of money. That's the measuring stick for respect in society. You could make crass roast videos filled with insults, and if you don't get a hundred thousand subscribers, if you don't make money, people would call you a loser, tell you to get a real job. But if you manage to get millions of subscribers, online gambling companies would give you brand deals; YouTube AdSense would rake in money; motivation gurus would invite you on their podcast to inspire the youth. In the same way, if I open a hundred branches of my tea shop, I would get invited to give motivational talks at IITs and IIMs. People would ask, "How did this wonderful idea come to you?" But if it's just one shop, then nobody would care.

But what if I become a famous artist and then open a tea shop? Then people would remark, "What a quirky, wild, crazy artist! Even after earning so much, he opened a tea shop. His mind is on another level entirely."

I remember reading somewhere that a famous writer used to work as a waiter in a restaurant. Not like in Bollywood stories, where they start off as a poor waiter and then become world-famous, telling journalists their sob stories, the camera panning to their tearful eyes, their parents' tears, their wife's tears, the audience's tears. Ugh, all the fun's gone thinking about it.

The story I heard was different– the writer had already become famous, had earned good money, and only after that did he start working as a waiter. When he was writing, he'd only write. The rest of the time, he'd work as a waiter somewhere. Maybe just for a few days. However long he wanted to– how cool is that! Maybe he'd always dreamt of working as a waiter in a restaurant for a while. My mom says I always talk like a madman. But only madmen can truly dream, right? Osho said that whether someone calls you a poet or a madman, it means the same thing. Ask them, "What did your logic ever get you anyway? Go, I bless you too– may you also go mad."

You need imagination to dream. Someone without imagination thinks that buying a Mercedes is a dream and the whole world agrees. Parents boast about it to neighbours and relatives while girlfriends preen over it. In such a scenario, genuine dreamers are bound to be called crazy.

Sonu would understand what I'm saying. That kid from Bihar who went viral in a bunch of videos; who said he wanted to become an IAS officer. Some local reporter asked him why. Sonu said he wanted to make India rank second in the world. The reporter asked, "Why not number one?" Sonu replied, "Because that's not my dream."

Everyone pretends that they want to make India rank one, and then they sell gutkha as cardamom. But Sonu dreamed of making the country rank second. IAS was a dream that his surroundings gave him, but the dream of making India rank second was truly his own. He didn't just repeat something rote. Something must have surely popped into his head. People who overthink won't get it. Because this isn't about thinking. It's a dream. Like the dreams you see in your sleep– anything can happen there!

And then when you wake up, that stunned feeling wraps you, "Wow, that was such a unique dream."

Dreams should be unique. But nowadays, everyone just dreams of a Mercedes, a bungalow, a swimming pool, expensive booze, business-class flights, and world tours–is that all? Is that it? Oh no, I almost forgot that Mickey Mouse place. Gotta take madam there too. Damn, is she a little kid?

And then people call 'Pyaasa' a tragic film. When your mind is full of this stuff, of course 'Pyaasa' feels tragic. Vijay says, "Even if I get the whole world, what's the point?" and he turns away all the fame. He leaves to live a peaceful life with his girlfriend. He'll still write poetry. The people who care about his poetry, not his fame, will still hear it. But he won't get tangled up in the trap. He says, "I am not Vijay," and walks away. What could be more of a happy ending than that? He's free from every burden.

What burden do I have? I don't have the pressure to get my sister married. I don't have to collect money for her dowry, because it's just the two of us brothers. I don't have to redeem my mom's pawned bangles, because she never pawned any. But mom did want a necklace once. Of course, a gold necklace with red beads. Did she ask me for it?

Honestly, I can't remember. She mentioned a necklace–something about her friend's son buying one for her. But my mom's so scared of wearing gold jewellery outside the house. Still, she might wear it to a party though. Maybe she never directly asked, but one day I would still get her that necklace. It's not a big deal. Even now, I have enough money in my account to buy it for her. Oh, but now I want to quit my job! I have to save up right now. If I buy her the necklace now and then ask her for money when I'm struggling, that would feel pretty bad. But I'll definitely get her the necklace, even if I don't become a famous artist. After four years of having quit this job, I'll earn at least that much, no matter what I do. Even by tutoring. By doing tiny roles in films. Doing theatre. Running a tea shop. I can promise her that much.

But I can't promise my girlfriend to show her the FIFA World Cup. Sometimes I feel like saying, "Are you a guest at a wedding procession or what?" But if I said that, the knife she's using to cut the apple right now, she'd use it on me. No, no, I'm joking. She gets angry, but she's not like that.

"Four years from now, we'll see if we go there or not. But for now, let's just watch the match. Are you not interested at all in the match?"

"Shut up. You've spoiled my mood completely. Do you even know what love is? Tried to talk a little romantic, and you set up a whole parliament debate instead. Can a person not even dream a little? You had to bring maths into it, too. Can't you just say 'alright' to make someone happy?"

"Dream as much as you want. But when you ask me to promise something, I'll have to do the math, right? Why don't you say that you'll take me to the next FIFA World Cup instead? You're earning too, you know."

"Yeah, it was my mistake. Sorry," she said, thumping both hands together in irritation.

Waving my hands, I said, "Alright, forgiven."

She got flustered for a second, then burst out laughing. Then, trying to bring her anger back again, she said, "It is pointless talking to you. I dream that in a few years, you'll be a famous artist. I'll quit my job and manage everything for you. I'll handle your meetings, your shoots, everything. If there's ever a poetry gathering at our house, you'll be wearing a white kurta-pajama with hand embroidery, and I'll put on a silk saree. I'll decorate the house before people arrive."

Jaun Elia was right–

> Whenever you come, you'll find me lost,
> In my solitude, there's nothing but dreams.
>
> You have a desire to decorate my room,
> In my room, there's nothing but books.
>
> तुम जब आओगी तो खोया हुआ पाओगी मुझे
> मेरी तन्हाई में ख़्वाबों के सिवा कुछ भी नहीं
>
> मेरे कमरे को सजाने की तमन्ना है तुम्हें
> मेरे कमरे में किताबों के सिवा कुछ भी नहीं

Continuing, she said, "These are the dreams I see for us. But you have to be realistic even about this! Oaths, promises– none of it matters to you."

"Promises do matter. That's why I don't want to make promises lightly."

For King Dasharath, a promise became the reason for his death. In the name of a vow, he gave two blank cheques to Kaikeyi. On one, Kaikeyi wrote Bharat's name for the throne, and on the other, exile for Ram.

King Bali promised Vaman dev three steps of land and got trapped. Vaman dev was actually Vishnu in disguise, who then grew in size with each step. He measured the sky in one step, the earth in the second, and placed the third on Bali's head, sending him to the underworld.

Karna also paid dearly for his promise. During the Mahabharat war, Indra disguised himself as a Brahmin and made Karna promise not to refuse any request. As soon as Karna agreed, Indra asked him for his armour and earrings, which made Karna invincible. Karna had to give them up.

The lesson is, of course, to keep your promises. But the bigger lesson is– don't easily make promises to anyone. In Shakespeare's play 'The Merchant of Venice,' Antonio almost had to give a pound of his flesh because Shylock lent him money under the contract that if Antonio couldn't pay back on time, he'd owe him a pound of flesh. Antonio's ships got delayed at sea, and he was preparing for his death. Thankfully, Portia played her hand well– she pointed out that the bond said only a pound of flesh, not a drop of blood, and if any blood were spilled, Shylock would also have to forfeit an equal amount. That saved Antonio; otherwise, a promise would have killed him.

Anyway, it's not like she would actually kill me, but she could definitely taunt me for life! "What happened to that promise of taking me to the FIFA World Cup, eh?" She'll tease me and then say, "Relax! I was just joking."

On top of that, I myself don't feel good if I make a promise and fail to keep it. Again, I told her that I'm not a politician who goes around making random promises. It's simple– if we have enough money, we'll go; otherwise, not. But I'm not going to change my whole life just to uphold this promise.

"Well, when did I ask you to give up on your dreams? All I meant was that if everything works out, we will go."

She hadn't actually said that. But I didn't feel like arguing anymore. So I said, "Okay."

That's how I successfully dodged the promise and started watching the match again, feeling relaxed. My dream stayed safe a while longer. There's always so much pressure on dreams– parents, society, marriage, your own ego, and of course, the pressure to go to the FIFA World Cup. As kids, we all dreamed unique dreams. But parents, school, TV, movies– they brainwash you; they implant society's collective 'dreams' into your mind. You end up trading your childhood dreams away. After a while, you even forget them. Do you remember what your dreams were?

When you were little
You thought,
You'd do something big.
You left for the big city,
Suitcase in hand,
Big dreams in your eyes.

You got into a big college,
From there, you landed
A big job at a big company,
Sat in a big office,
Became a big officer,
Got a big salary.

You bought a big house,
And a big car,
A big TV, a big bed,
A big sofa, a big bar,
An expensive single malt in it.
You work out too
At a big gym,
Your kids go to
A big school.
Everything is so big,
So why do you grumble?
Wherein came the trouble,
That changes form,
But never goes away–
That craving on weekends for big fun,
But then, you get bored and look for
A tiny corner of peace,
Where you can lay down on a rug
And find some rest for your soul.

But you already made that trade, right?
The one big dream you had,

The one linked to society,
Filled with innocence,
With passion, with drive,
With the urge to be a superhero,
To be the savior of the oppressed,
The friend of all friends -
Remember what that was?
Maybe it was to be
A journalist who raised people's issues,
Or a godlike doctor saving lives,
Or a great musician,
Or maybe a lawyer fighting for justice,
Or a police officer taking down criminals.

You had some big dream like that,
The dream you traded away.
Traded away your conscience, your innocence,
In exchange for a big house, a big car.
You chose to
Eat, drink, shop on weekends,
And spend the other five days
Dying a little each day,
Stressed out,
Calling this sorry state
The truth of life.

When did you make that trade?
Was it when you took that job?

Got into college?
Maybe even before that,
When you started going
To coaching centers in 11th grade?
Don't feel ashamed today,
Tell the truth -
When did you sell out?

Because it's not possible
That since childhood,
Your dream really was
To bend knee to the powerful as a journalist,
Become a rich doctor
Doing unnecessary heart surgery
For fat commissions,
Or to clear the jungle to build a factory,
Or argue in court to save a murderer,
No kid dreams of being the lazy teacher
Who ruins the future of the nation,
Or being the politician or officer
Who bleeds the people dry,
Or being a singer who makes crass songs,
Or a famous actor advertising gutkha.

No child says,
"I have no social responsibility"
Children dream of being Superman,
And saving the whole world.

I've never seen a kid
Whose soul was devoured
By greed for money.

Think back -
What forced you?
Why did you make that deal?
Or did someone else steal your dream
Back in childhood?
Was it some elder
Who made that trade for you?
To be absorbed in work you love,
To lose yourself completely -
Someone replaced that
With the fun of consumption,
Stole away your raw, innocent dreams
And implanted these "big" dreams,
Empty of any greatness.
Who made the deal-

You or someone else?
When and why-
If you can't remember,
That's okay.

There's still time,
Dream again.
How long will you suffocate
In these cement palaces?
Come out.

There is no place
You can't turn back from.
Stop searching for
Some tiny corner of peace -
There's a whole world
Overflowing with peace
Waiting for you.
Just look for it,
You'll find some path
To reach there.

Chapter -2

The Golden Cage

Watching the football match was fun. It always is. It's not just about sidestepping my girlfriend; Honestly, sports matches just look better on TV. Hockey, cricket, football, or tennis - it doesn't matter. Watch it with your girlfriend, with your family, or with your friends. Everyone yells together - 'Yayyyy, goal!' Some of my friends watch it while drinking beer. Yeah, I know that beer is bad for your health. The ones who don't drink beer, they have cola. Well, that's unhealthy too. Whatever, you could have cold coffee. Eat some popcorn. If you want to have beer or cola, that's your choice. Besides, you don't have to be munching on something all the time. Watch with full focus, without any distractions. Watch lying on your sofa or sitting on a chair.

A lot of restaurants have big screens set up. There, drinks and snacks are expensive. But it still costs less than flying to another country just to see the match.

Once, I watched a cricket match at Feroz Shah Kotla stadium, and honestly, it didn't feel like I was missing out on something special. But if you really want to feel it for yourself, go to any random match, why the World Cup. It's not just about international flights. Hotel prices in those cities soar high during such big events. When the

Cricket World Cup was held in Ahmedabad, rooms that usually cost 3-4 thousand rupees were being booked for 20 thousands. Somewhere else, it rose to 50 thousand. In five-star hotels, rates shot up to rupees 2 lakhs.

When Coldplay had a concert in Mumbai, tickets were being sold in the black market. It was the same situation in every Mumbai hotel. For one night, prices reached 1-1.5 lakh rupees. You might say, "This is a free market," but what kind of free market is it when you can't even get a cheap room, and your only freedom is to pick which expensive hotel you want? If capitalism is going to blackmail me like this and rob me under the name of supply and demand, I'm not cool with this. Why should anyone accept this kind of scam?

But we're okay with everything. We've just accepted that the world is like this; this is how things are. Movie tickets are always ranging between 300 and 400 rupees. A water bottle that costs 20 rupees outside is on sale for 80 rupees in cinema halls. If you go with your girlfriend, you have to spend 300 on popcorn and a cola. If you go to the movies with your family, you end up spending 2,500.

In companies, working 12-13 hours a day is normal. Target and deadline pressures are normal. It is usual for jobs to be boring. The boss will always yell at you. You keep going back and forth from home to office. Traffic jams along the way are normal. You keep saying that you go home only to sleep - and accept that this is how it is. There's just no time for family.

Where houses are cheap, there are no jobs. Where there are jobs, houses are always expensive. You have to take a loan. You have to pay the EMIs. You have to have a car. You need a separate loan for the car, because whatever money you have, you always end up buying a car slightly out of your budget. You have to buy an expensive phone. You have to change your phone every 2-3 years. Cities are always polluted. Roads are always dirty. This is how the things are.

When the water got bad, we installed water purifiers. When the air got bad, we bought air purifiers. Sleeper coaches in trains kept getting worse. There's not even soap outside train toilets. Should a poor person not wash their hands with soap? Are their bodies so different that they don't even need hygiene? Whatever, we just started traveling in AC 3-Tier. When those became too crowded, we switched to Second AC or First AC. And if you don't get a seat there, then just fly. When there were potholes on the road, we bought expensive cars so that we'd feel the bumps less. There is no time for exercise, so now we take so many regular pills for gas, blood pressure etc., that we have memorized the names of these medicines.

Government hospitals are overcrowded, don't treat us properly. So we started going to private hospitals. It is normal for treatments to be expensive there. Government schools got worse, so we started sending our kids to private schools. It is normal for their monthly fees to be 15-20 thousand. You have to pay a donation. College fees for private institutes are in lakhs. You have to take a student loan for education. Most colleges aren't IITs or IIMs. Still, they're expensive. Medical college fees are always 50-60 lakhs. In some colleges, it is more than a crore!

Schools, hospitals, roads, cleanliness – we get nothing much in terms of government services, but still we have to pay tax on everything. Salaries don't increase, but prices always do. Politicians are always corrupt. Political party tickets are up for sale. Money is spent like water in elections. MLAs are on sale. They spend money to win the election, and then recover money from us after winning. The companies that donated to the election campaigns get special favors. Every other day, there is news about fake medicines. The world is just like this. This is just how life goes. We'll handle it. We'll never ask why.

Every citizen in a democracy should be asking that question. But we vote once every five years and then step aside. We've given ourselves a permanent certificate of helplessness. We've memorized these lines -

"What difference will my words make?"

"I don't know about my own life, how can I worry about the country?"

"This country can't be fixed."

"What can people like us even do?"

If we chase our dreams, become a singer, maybe perform at some restaurant-bar, we'll make 40,000 per month. But deep down, we know -

"What's 40,000 these days anyway? To live a decent life, you need at least one lakh a month."

We know it's all messed up; only 1-2% of people earn that kind of money. But we hope to be among that 1-2%. Who cares about the rest of the country!

In the film 'Zanjeer,' Vijay is an honest police inspector. His wife Mala shows him a picture of a beautiful house. She says, when they build a new home, she'll put up curtains like that. Driven by his restlessness, Vijay bursts out–

> "We'll put up beautiful curtains in our home. And I won't even try to find out what's happening in the world outside those curtains. If people die outside our lovely home, so be it. If smugglers' cars run over little kids outside, what does it matter to me! I promise you, Mala, if I ever hear their screams, I'll close my ears... Yes, Mala, we will definitely build a beautiful home, and we'll forget how ugly the outside world is. We'll forget the injustice, the cruelty - we'll forget all of it."

That's what we're trying to do. We're just trying to climb to a position in this system where we don't have to endure anything. Where some rich guy's Porsche doesn't run us over; where we don't die falling into an open manhole while riding our motorcycle; where our home doesn't get wiped out by floods or storms; where the flames of a riot don't reach us. We want our home in a posh apartment complex with gates, fences, and security guards.

We've accepted that someone is bound to be exploited; our only concern is that it should not be us. That's why we want to climb to the top of the pyramid - by becoming a politician, a government officer, or just earning a ton of money. And if that means having to work in a toxic job, we'll do it. Even if it means we must be stressed, lose sleep, choke our own dreams to death. We'll do it all, and then we'll say: "This is life's reality. This is just how it is. Dreams just get left behind."

In this worn-out life, for entertainment, we'll go to restaurant-bars, wash off a week's worth of boredom, go shopping, put on a show for Instagram, watch IPL matches, or take that one holiday trip a year. No matter how much that Thailand-Malaysia trip costs - that's what we earn for, isn't it?

While doing all this, our objective is to somehow shift to another country. In our country, the measure of success is to have left the country, to have settled abroad. From the Prime Minister to your relatives, everyone will respect you. While living there, we'll say that we miss our country. It's not just drama; you really do miss home. But if we had to leave our country to access basic facilities, and had to give up our unique dreams, then how is that our fault? We've suffered so much ourselves. We worked 70 hours a week just to reach abroad; only then did the company give us this chance.

We keep saying that this is a rat race. But we keep running in it. We keep running to get into a golden cage. 'Passenger' said something amazing in his song 'Life Is For The Living'–

"They take your dreams down
and stick them in storage
You can have them back son
when you've paid off
Your mortgage and loans

Oh hell with this place,
I'll go it my own way
I'll stick out my thumb
and I trudge down the highway"

We like such songs, we love movies like '3 Idiots,' but then we tell ourselves - after all, it's just a movie. We think that no matter what the film says, success won't just follow us around in real life, and that's absolutely true.

Fine. Phunsuk Wangdu had a brilliant mind, he was really interested in science, and became a scientist with 400 patents to his name. But even Farhan also becomes a successful wildlife photographer. Four of his books get published. Raju, who was a duffer at studies, also becomes a successful researcher, becomes a blogger. Everyone has loads of money. Happy ending. Applause.

We really like the movie, but it's not enough to make us quit our jobs or have the guts to break out of this trap. Doubts start popping up in our heads - who even buys wildlife photography books? You can see as many wildlife photos on Google as you want.

Maybe it's a rich people's thing - dad's a millionaire, son buys a ₹10 lakh lens and camera, books tickets to Kenya, comes back with lion pictures, books an art gallery for an exhibition, some millionaire buys a photo for lakhs, some wildlife magazine buys another for lakhs. Is that how it is? We don't know.

In the movie '*Tamasha*,' Ved discovers his real identity. His dad doesn't understand, so he explains it to him. And boom! he straight up becomes a Broadway star. The audience claps at his play. We, the viewers, also clap. We get all motivated. But then we think - sure, we know our real identity, and maybe dad would agree, but could we really become an accomplished actor? Could we earn money doing theatre?

We hear Nawazuddin Siddiqui's success story. We get all fired up. But then we see a scene from 'Munna Bhai M.B.B.S.' (2003), where he played a tiny role of a pickpocket. In an interview, Nawaz said that while doing that scene, he was only thinking, "Hope I get paid after this." Why?

"Because I used to be so hungry back then. I never had any money. So in my head all I could think was, as soon as this is over, someone will hand me a cheque or some cash, and I'll finally eat a full meal."

Then we remember the '*Sarfarosh*' (1999) jail scene, where Aamir Khan's character is beating up Nawaz's character. Nawaz got his big break in 2012's 'Gangs of Wasseypur' - that's thirteen years after his first movie. Such a long struggle?

But wait, didn't Rajkummar Rao get a role much quicker? But will we? Dad used to say, "Thousands, even lakhs of people struggle in Mumbai. Only a handful ever make it big." Back then, we were only 18 and had to listen to dad. But now there's nothing stopping us from sending that resignation email. Now all those things sound practical. We love dancing, but the same question pops up in our head - the one dad asked - what's the scope in this? His voice still echoes in our ears, "Son, hobbies won't pay the bills."

But then we watch Neeraj Chopra win an Olympic gold medal, and the longing stirs inside again. Then comes another motivational story - KFC's founder started his restaurant at 44; he opened his first franchise at 62. We get filled with motivation all over again.

But while we're struggling, how do we survive in the meantime? And what about the EMIs for the house, the car, the phone? Let's save up a bit first. But how much? Let's say at least 25 lakh rupees. By then, we'll be of marriageable age, then kids, then their expenses. By then we're used to saying, "I too once dreamed of doing something, but never got the right circumstances. I just got stuck in the daily grind."

Of course, we can manage our daily bread and butter, but we do like a bit of paneer butter masala and matar mushroom as well. Maybe we don't talk about it in front of others, but we sure enjoy the perks. And it feels good to get attention, likes on Instagram. It gives us social status. People rush to shake hands with us. Neighbors and relatives use us as a living example for their own kids - "Be like him, look at this wonderful job, how much he earns, what an awesome car he bought." Consuming things and getting attention - it really does feel good.

Maybe you'll think, wow, this is exactly what I feel - but the truth is that millions relate to this. Which means quitting a job isn't just a personal thing - it's a social one. Not just a chain, but a web. A finely-woven trap. A matrix.

This matrix has fancy restaurants. I ate in every expensive restaurant in Connaught Place; went with friends too. Once I saw a pair of brick-red coloured shoes in a shop's showcase and liked them right away. After trying those on, I asked the salesperson to pack them up.

For the first time ever, I asked the price after getting something packed. Six thousand rupees? Here, swipe my card. Using your debit card is extra thrilling in the beginning. With cash, you see it leaving your hand; a card feels like Aladdin's lamp - just swipe it on the machine and your wish comes true.

One day mom said, "I am putting on weight; we should have a weighing machine at home." The next day, she saw it sitting there. The office bus would take me to the office and back, but sometimes if I got late, they would provide me a cab. Dad was so happy about this.

I went traveling with friends from the office. We went rafting somewhere high above Rishikesh. There's a cliff from where you can jump straight into the water. I was scared the first time, but then I jumped thrice.

I had '*Ghamandi Lassi*' in Indore. That's the name of a shop there. The company had sent me there on work. Ranbaxy - the biggest pharma company in India. My job was to manage the supply chain. The production plant was in Dewas, near Indore. This two-week plant visit was part of my training.

The company's guest house had no vacancies. So they put me up at a hotel, booked me a suite! I'd never even heard the word before. When I walked in, there was a drawing room first, with sofas and a TV. Then, past a divider, there was a bedroom. The room even had a fridge. I called the HR lady to say, "Ma'am, everything looks amazing, thank you!" She said, "No need to thank me, you deserve this."

There was a bathtub in the bathroom. I love bathing. A cold bath in summer. A hot bath in winter. Bathing in the rain. Bathing in a tube-well tank. Bathing in a river, in a waterfall. And now, added to my list was bathing in a bathtub.

As I was getting out of the tub, I saw a towel lying on the floor. There was a separate towel for drying yourself. I picked up the one on the floor and hung it up.

I woke up late in the morning; got ready in a rush; when I got back from the office in the evening, I saw that the housekeeping had cleaned the whole room. My clothes, which I'd thrown around in the morning in a hurry, were neatly folded. The towel was again lying on the bathroom floor. Actually, I should say that the towel was placed on the floor. Just like the previous day. Why's that? Someone from the staff told me that when you step out of the bathtub, the water dripping off your body gets soaked up by this floor towel. I'd heard of doormats, but this was the first time I'd heard about floor towels.

Just like breakfast, dinner was a buffet too. Ten types of dishes; eat whatever you want. I got up to get extra dal in a bowl, and when I came back to the table, my plate was gone. Some waiter had taken it away. And I was still in the middle of eating. Could they not have asked me? When I spoke to a waitress, she explained, "Sir, if you get up in the middle of your meal, just cross your fork and spoon on the plate. If you've finished eating, place them straight, side by side."

Now I am learning rich people's etiquette! After three-four days, I shifted to the company guest house. That place was sparkling too.

On my way back from Indore, I traveled by air for the first time. I was flying among the clouds. The air hostess asked me, "Sir, would you like something to eat?" There was a sandwich for 150 rupees, which you'd get outside for 15-20 bucks. So what? It was all on the company's dime.

As people often say - "The money's good, but the company totally sucks the life out of you" - well, that wasn't true in my case. I know this takes some drama out of my story. It's more fun when there's more struggle in a story. Like a person full of fragrant dreams, stuck in a company where he has to work 15-16 hours a day, getting yelled at by the boss, but forced by circumstance to put up with it. Will he get out? That's more dramatic, more relatable too. Because many companies really do have such a toxic work culture.

We see it in the news. Many of my friends have told me their bitter experiences.

But I'll not say that Ranbaxy was sucking my blood, because in my case, that wasn't the truth. The office bus would drop us at work in the morning and bring us back in the evening. So, fixed hours– 9:00 to 5:30. The company provided lunch for everyone. Hot, healthy, and delicious food. Roti, two to three types of veggies, dal, rice, dessert, salad, papad. Sometimes Indian, sometimes American style, sometimes Italian. The lunch mattered to me because tiffin boxes have always felt like a scam to me. I feel that once people used to work from home; then they were called into factories, into companies; hot meals were snatched from them and replaced with tiffin boxes. If anyone protested, the office installed a microwave in which you can reheat your food. But in my company, we got fresh, hot lunch.

The workload wasn't crazy either. Like I said, fixed hours. Only sometimes I'd have to stay late. But it wasn't like you'd imagine, with a mound of files on my desk, me rubbing my eyes and staring at the computer screen all night, super stressed out. No, it wasn't like that. Once a month, I'd have to run some software for planning. I'd feed in the data, and then the software did all the work– cranking out reports for hours. I just had to check it periodically to make sure everything was running smoothly. If the software stopped, I'd fix any errors and restart the run. So when all that was happening, I could just wander around the empty office. I could order dinner, have coffee or tea. I could even read novels.

I hardly ever had to go to work on weekends– maybe just two or three times. Though, one such working weekend was when the company had a big annual celebration for all the employees, and I was the only one not there. But never mind. In the company, and especially on our team, parties were common. A joining party for someone. A farewell party. Birthday parties. And every now and then, just a party because it had been too long without one.

My boss was a fantastic person. He wasn't like Narayan Murthy, making people work 70 hours a week. He understood that happy employees are more productive. So whatever budget the company allotted for team-building, he used it well. For lunch, sometimes we'd be at Barbeque Nation, sometimes at a famous dhaba on the highway.

There was always laughter and jokes. Sometimes I'd recite one of my poems, and everyone would listen carefully and praise me. We'd talk about movies. My boss was the one who recommended that I should watch 'Aakrosh' and 'Ardh Satya'– outstanding films. He also gave me a book by Jiddu Krishnamurti.

While we joked around, we'd also end up discussing the company's strategy. The others had many more years of experience than me, but they'd still ask what I thought. Like, what changes could we make in software queries or algorithms to boost efficiency.

Including me, four people from my college and seven from another college were recruited together. After training, we were placed in various departments. If you ever went to the company's plant, you were treated with respect– ah, you're from the corporate office! And in the corporate headquarters itself, the eleven of us again got special treatment, like we were the young warriors, the future of the company. We got to meet the Chief Information Officer– the head of IT at Ranbaxy. During training, we got exposure to every department.

I did make one blunder at work once, but apart from that, I did pretty well. Within two to three months, I was given responsibility for a module of the software. Two people worked under my supervision. There was a critical overhaul, replacing our planning and optimization software with a new one, and I played a significant role in that.

And this wasn't about selling cola drinks or anything; this was about medicines. So it also felt good that my company was doing something meaningful for society. Supplying quality medicines at low prices not just in India, but in other countries too.

So overall, the salary was good. The work was meaningful, and I was doing it well. One didn't have to slog like a donkey; the hours were fixed. Along with work, there were parties. There was no jealousy among colleagues. The boss was supportive.

There was even a chance to go to America. You might be thinking that all of this sounds perfect. So then why did I want to quit the job? Think about it.

Have you forgotten that I had a dream? The dream of becoming an artist. If you forgot my dream, that's understandable. People often forget their own dreams, or want to forget them. Honestly, maybe it's better for some people to just forget their dreams. Some folks ask me, "Should I quit my job to get into films?" I tell them straight-up, no. They ask me because they're scared. But scared of what? Starving? No, they come from families where even if they never earned another rupee, they wouldn't starve. They have their own house, car, property, bank balance, and their spouse earns too.

If someone is really the only breadwinner in the family, parents living in slums, living in a rented place in another city, wife and kids totally dependent - and if they don't earn for a few months, they'll struggle just to eat, then they shouldn't quit. Their fear is justified.

But those who ask me about quitting aren't scared of losing food, clothing, shelter. So what are they scared of? The trap we talked about - it has its comforts. The fun of consumption and the attention from society. How do you leave this house of reality behind for a bungalow of dreams? What if you end up with neither? That's scary, right?

Siddharth didn't get scared. He'd lived in palaces since birth, surrounded by every luxury. He never experienced hardship. Then one day, he left the palace and saw an old man, a sick man, and a corpse. Some Buddhist texts say he didn't actually see these things, but just thought about them.

Whatever the case, something inside him stirred; questions came up that he wanted the answers to; he wanted a cure for human suffering. In Buddhist terminology, he was filled with '*samvega*' - a sort of spiritual urgency for depth in life. He left the palace for the forest. Did he fret about how he'd live in the forest? No. At that point, staying in the palace was the thing that made him restless.

People ask me what the film industry is like. I tell them straight. It's not easy. It'll mess with your head. If someone has that '*samvega*', they won't be stopped by this warning. If they're stopped, then clearly they're missing that drive. Their fear isn't about losing food, clothing, or shelter - that'll be there - but the fear is about losing all this fun. Quitting your job isn't just a personal or social decision - it's a spiritual one too.

So can you see that maybe my story actually has more drama than you thought? There weren't thorns stuck to my office chair pricking me all the time. Life was easy. That's exactly why there was nothing pushing me to leave.

Leaving a golden cage can be harder than leaving an iron one. If the salary isn't much, people can convince themselves thinking, "What am I really earning here anyway?" Nawazuddin once said in an interview that acting was the only thing he knew, so that's what he had to do. He didn't expect to get a film role in Mumbai, but he thought - what do I have to lose anyway?

Similarly, if the work culture is toxic, it's easy for someone to get frustrated and think– I'm done with this job where I can't even get a moment's peace. But if the salary is high, and the work culture isn't toxic, then there's more at stake. So people get more confused.

But confusion is in the mind, while passion is in the heart. When your heart is pulling you somewhere, all the confusion in your head just vanishes. That's how you break out of golden cages. That's the path to wanderlust, to adventure. I had that drive inside me. There was a wave rising in my heart.

In just a few months, I started to feel like I'd indulged enough. I'd enjoyed the luxuries of the rich, eaten at expensive restaurants, worn fancy clothes, now what? Is this what my life is going to be forever? No, I wasn't okay with that. I'd tasted real joy back in college. That's the joy I wanted.

Chapter -3

The Quest

A lot of people say they've never found their passion. They don't really feel enthusiastic about anything. The good thing is that at least, they realize this. If they look for it, they'll definitely find it one day.

But does passion really come from searching for it? If someone had a childhood dream, does that always turn into passion as they grow older? Not necessarily, because those dreams are often dismissed with remarks like:

"In childhood, every kid dreams about all sorts of things. If a child sees an airplane, he wants to be a pilot. After watching a sci-fi movie, he thinks of becoming an astronaut. He watches some drama films and wants to be an actor. Hears a song and wishes to be a singer. But kids have limited exposure. What do they know about real life? Life isn't a dream."

These comments don't just come from parents and society, but often from people themselves, looking back at their own childhood dreams. And, to be fair, it makes some sense. It's true that a child's exposure is limited.

That's why it's important to give children exposure. Tell them that:

- The dinosaur movie you're watching is about real creatures that once walked the earth. We know this from studying fossils. The people who do this work are called paleontologists.
- Paleontologists often work with archaeologists, who excavate sites. There, they may find fossils, skeletons, ruins of ancient villages, sculptures, tools, arrows, and who knows what else. By studying these findings, they figure out how life used to be in ancient times.
- Historians study written materials from the past to understand history.
- Kids should be told that the symbol on their shoes is a company logo, a kind of brand mark. It helps identify the company without using its name. There are designers who put much thought into creating it.
- Your clothes have been designed by fashion designers.
- The food you eat was grown by a farmer. Take kids to a farm sometimes; let them plant something with their own hands.
- Show them how jaggery peanut brittle (gajjak) is made; how chocolate is produced; how biscuits are baked in a bakery.
- Teach geography by having them solve the jigsaw puzzle of the world map.
- Schools should have guest lectures where environmentalists like Mahesh Chandra Mehta share their adventures, like how he saved the Taj Mahal from acid rain.

- Imagine 9th and 10th graders from a hundred schools gathered in a stadium, where a Nobel prize-winning economist like Abhijit Banerjee explains his work and what earned him the prize.
- A scientist could share his interesting invention stories and run science workshops for kids.
- If it's not possible to bring scientists or economists to every school, do it via video conference, or show pre-recorded videos. There could be documentaries on various topics for kids.
- Schools could have a cinema room to show the best of world cinema.
- Sometimes take kids to museums. Take them to art galleries and let them freely express what they feel about a painting. Take them to plays. Invite a singer to the school who can explain the difference between genres like Thumri, Khayal, Dadra, Hori, Ghazal, Dhrupad.

Right now, not much of this really happens. If kids don't know about paleontologists, how would they ever dream of becoming one? A child might enjoy watching birds but has no idea what an ornithologist is. Some listen to others carefully, can almost read minds - they might make good psychologists, but how would they know?

Some have a detective mind; they're good at investigating. Some argue well with logic, like seasoned lawyers. Some kids love animals. Some are fascinated by tiny insects, butterflies, spiders. Some love forests, mountains, oceans.

But none of this guides their dreams, because they don't know that these careers exist.

They choose dreams based on what they see and understand around them. Actor, singer, dancer, cricketer, pilot, army officer, police, computer engineer, doctor. Or maybe their dream is to own a Mercedes, Porsche, BMW, or a Jaguar. Watching music videos and vlogs, kids have started dreaming about cars too. They'll say, "I'm passionate about cars."

In this sense, aren't children's dreams - and later, leaving those dreams behind - just a part of the same web we've talked about? So if a parent says, "Stop chasing childhood dreams and get serious," is that really wrong? They too are just part of the same web.

When they say this, you might agree: "Yeah, forget it, that was just childhood stuff." But actually, the solution should be that if you didn't get exposure as a kid, at least make sure that now you get it.

A quick Google search can pull up the full list of careers. AI can give you all kinds of info on any career. If you tell AI about your interests, skills, personality, and values, it can even suggest some careers suitable for you.

On YouTube, there are international podcasts where experts from all kinds of fields - paleontologists, ornithologists, theoretical physicists, statisticians, data scientists - are interviewed. These might only get 8-10 thousand views, so they won't show up in your YouTube feed. They're outside your web. You'll have to seek them out.

Even if you're not looking for a new career, you can at least be informed; connect with the world to know what kinds of work exist; and eventually, give your kids more exposure.

Who knows, maybe you'll find something that really interests you; you'll dig deeper, and it'll turn into a passion. Maybe you get so drawn in that you decide this is what you want to do. You might undergo a course while working, and eventually switch careers. To do something different, first you have to know what's even possible.

But aside from lack of exposure, there's another problem. You're used to following instructions– from parents, teachers, bosses– since childhood. But if you quit your job and go freelance, or start your own business, nobody gives you instructions then. You have to motivate yourself, decide how much you'll work, and when to rest. You have to go out and look for work. That means sending emails, networking. Whether you're an editor, a music composer, or a website designer, you need to find clients. You'll need to learn how to create a Google Business Profile, run ads on Instagram, and register your business on search engines, like Just Dial.

If you open your own salon, café, tiffin service, boutique, or a photo studio, you'll need to attract customers. Even if you hire people for marketing, sales, branding, product design, manufacturing, or service, you still have to make the big plan yourself.

Were you ever trained in all this? No. Forget school; even if you did an MBA, most of the time you were just prepped to take a job.

So whether it's limited exposure or the habit of taking instructions, you end up stuck. That's why the decision to quit your job isn't just a personal, social, or spiritual one– it's a psychological decision too. You have to rewire your entire mindset.

Otherwise, if you make decisions with your same old constrained way of thinking, is it even really a decision? For example, say someone goes to a restaurant. He's been going there for ten years. Every single time, he orders upma and filter coffee. The waiters know this, but still ask, "What would you like to eat today?"

There's a new chef. The waiter places a 50-rupee wager with him: the chef says that the man will order uttapam; the waiter says he'll order upma and filter coffee. Technically, this guy could order anything, but he chooses upma and filter coffee, just like always. Is that really a choice? Or is he just trapped by habit, by his nature, his likes and dislikes?

In the same way, someone who's used to being instructed since childhood will get nervous about freelancing. That anxiety makes them choose to stay in a job, or never quit a job. But was that ever really a choice? Or is it all just an illusion?

At this point, we're brushing up against that whole 'free will' debate, but let's not go down that road yet. Intellectuals might say that free will is theoretically impossible. Let them debate; this isn't the time for it. What is freedom, what is will? We'll get into all that in the 'Control Your Destiny' ebook.

For now, just think about this: a person stays stuck if they're stuck; and if they're moving, they just keep going in the same direction, unless some outside force acts on them. And by 'outside', I don't just mean someone else. I mean something outside your entire web.

Even your parents' way of raising you is part of your system. If they're salaried people, you get nervous about starting a business. If they're business people, you're more comfortable with it. If you heard your mom practising music, you started humming too. If your dad's a lawyer, that makes law a possible career option for you. Your economic situation, neighborhood, friends, culture– it's all part of your web. Wrestlers bring Olympic medals to Haryana, and the kids there try to make a name in wrestling. Hyderabad turns into an IT hub, so kids there want to become IT engineers.

Poet Waseem barelvi says:

> Since home learning came in the hands of TV,
> No child now steps in the shoes of their father.
>
> घरों की तर्बियत क्या आ गई टीवी के हाथों में
> कोई बच्चा अब अपने बाप के ऊपर नहीं जाता

Here, he's talking about the massive influence of TV, cinema, and mass media. Like we said before: watch an IPL match on TV, and cricket becomes appealing. Watch a movie hero in a cop's uniform, and you want to join the police. See fancy cars in music videos, and now you want one too.

It is said that YouTube gives you suggestions in your feed, but actually, YouTube tells you straight up that your feed is personalized as per your preferences. Watch one random influencer, and YouTube immediately serves up another influencer just like them. Listen to a song once, and your feed fills up with similar tunes. Ads on your profile work the same way– check out a T-shirt once and suddenly it's all T-shirt ads.

If your parents never listened to classical music, and your school never played it, then you are not interested in it. YouTube showed you trending Punjabi pop songs, FM radio played you the same songs– you started listening, and those became your favorites. Whether it's movies or music, if you've only consumed fast-paced stuff, your attention span adapted accordingly. They say that a person is a product of their environment; it's true.

All this is just part of your web now, and it's become part of your mind too. The ideas in your society, the political climate, the cultural atmosphere, your personal circumstances– it's all shaped your mind.

So what's "outside"? You must have heard it before: try something new. That's a fun idea. "New" doesn't have to mean what's new on the market; it means what's actually new to you.

In a restaurant, a guy saw someone at a side table eating podi idli. He told the waiter, "Whatever that is, bring me the same." This time, the waiter lost his bet. You might say that if someone has never wanted to try something new their whole life, why would they start now? That's the point. That's the trap.

There will be an effort to spread this message to the world– 'try something new', but since we're already talking about it here, at least you could think about it while visiting a restaurant next time.

It doesn't matter that he liked the podi idli more or less than the upma. Odds are, he liked it less, because the taste of upma has been stamped on his tongue for years. What matters is that he tried something new.

If you always stick to your preferences, you'll only ever do the same things you've always done. To see something new, you have to step outside your preferences, step outside your web. No one's going to just hand you a plate and say, "Here, try something new." You'll have to seek it out yourself. A beverage made from buransh flowers, kokum sharbat, solkadhi, tea with timur seeds, and so many other unique things are out there.

But people, even when they travel to a new place, they stay at a hotel, visit some sightseeing spots, and that's it– back they go. They go as tourists and return as tourists. Even at a new place, if they find Maggi or their regular paneer butter masala, that's what they opt for. If they have to eat local food because there's nothing familiar, they get irritated instead of savoring the experience. They don't talk to the local people, show no interest in the local music, dance, or theatre. Even after going to a new place, they avoid anything new; forget searching for something new by themselves.

But the question is, if we're talking about careers, why are we talking about new foods? Why new movies, or different music? Why try new things in every field? What's the connection to your career?

I have a friend who organizes film screenings. He runs a film club with a membership fee. If people show up to these screenings without being members, they have to buy tickets. Sometimes they charge some filmmaker for screening his movie and then, the revenue is shared. He collaborates with cultural centers and some cafés for these screenings.

What kind of films does he screen? Obviously, he won't screen movies starring Salman Khan. He wouldn't get permission, and also, it wouldn't make sense. Those movies are for multiplexes and OTT platforms. He screens rare films– world cinema, independent Indian films, stuff like that. It's not like he was into artistic films since childhood– that's not possible. His parents weren't interested in cinema. He came from a poor family, exposed only to mainstream stuff. But one day, someone suggested he try watching a different kind of film. After that, he watched more, realized that these were films others should watch too, and started doing screenings. It turned into a sustainable model.

Similarly, someone tried amaranth and found out that it's an ancient, nutritious Indian grain. They got a farmer to grow it, started packing and selling it on Amazon. It's not like they ate amaranth as a kid, but one day they tried it. Some village guy tried pasta and thought, "Hey, village kids might like this too," so he started making pasta locally.

The point isn't that you have to try out new cuisines only if you are thinking of a food-related business. No, it's a whole mental framework. You need an open mind. Even if you're not going to work in movies, watch new kinds of films anyway– they'll give you fresh ideas.

Most of the people who've seen 'Into the Wild' or 'Fight Club' will admit that these films stirred something inside. It's not that you become Tyler Durden right after watching 'Fight Club'; there are a lot of other factors at play. One film alone can't break the web, but it can help.

Motivational stories often talk about people who survived road accidents and had an epiphany, then completely re-examined their lives. But hey, you're not going to wait to have an accident, right? If a film or poem sparks something in you, isn't that wonderful?

Tyler Durden says, "You are not your job. You are not your bank balance. You are not your car."

In the movie 'Into the Wild', Chris says he doesn't want a new car. And it's not sour grapes; his wealthy parents are gifting him one. When he says that his current car works fine, he doesn't need a new one, he doesn't want all this stuff. All these things, things, things– he's sick of it. He wants to smash that typical American web of life and thus hits the road.

'American Beauty' won five Oscars, including Best Picture. The character Lester decides he's going to start living his life. He quits his dead-end job. His wife Carolyn embodies that American dream where a $4,000 Italian silk sofa equals a successful life. But for Lester, the meaning of life has changed now.

In 'Revolutionary Road', Frank doesn't know what his passion is, but he knows he doesn't want the job he's in. His wife April offers that they move to Paris, so he can discover his passion. But right then, his company offers him a promotion.

In the film 'Dharavi', Rajkaran is a taxi driver who wants to escape from his life of poverty, struggling to break free.

These films are not about quitting your job– they're about breaking the web. For a film to touch you, it must have depth. Books and poems can stir your soul, but only if you actually read them.

But if that's not your taste, how will you ever read those books? And if you never read them, how will you develop that taste? Now that we've talked about it, the idea is to step outside your likes and dislikes and try something new. Watch outstanding cinema. Read good books that make you think, that hold a mirror to you, that soar in your imagination and make your every nerve tingle.

Reading, in itself, is an act that activates your mind. When you start thinking, you start asking questions. When people say, "That's just how it is," you ask, "But why is it that way?"

There's a popular quote online: "The problem with the world is that fools are full of certainty, while intelligent people are full of doubts." But if you really look at it, that's not a problem; a person is intelligent precisely because they've left space for doubt. A fool reads something on WhatsApp and thinks they've discovered some deep truth, especially if it confirms what they already believe. People love to see their own ideas validated. Having read a WhatsApp message, they're filled with confidence that they know this while others don't. They never doubt that maybe this is not true. And that's just a WhatsApp forward which they read just now; there is no question of doubting the ideas that have been in their head for years.

The intelligent person asks questions. They're open to questions from others too. If anything they believe is found to be wrong, they update their knowledge; they change their behavior; that's how they improve. Most stubborn people, on the other hand, are unwilling to listen or understand anything different. That's why doubt is powerful. Asking questions can make you revolutionary.

Why can't girls study? Jyotiba Phule and Savitribai Phule didn't just accept "That's just how it is"; they questioned it. Savitribai, with her friend Fatima Sheikh, started teaching girls. Conservative folks would throw tomatoes, eggs, even cow dung at them. Savitribai would carry an extra sari for the walk to school.

Why can't Dalits touch the water of the village pond? Dr. Ambedkar questioned it, led the Mahad Satyagraha, went to Chaavdar Pond with many Dalits, and drank the water.

Questioning can make you a scientist. If you toss something up, it falls back to the ground– why? Newton asked and discovered gravity.

Questioning frees you from any web; it frees you from the web of "That's just how it is."

If you really explore the world, you're bound to find something

- that excites you, that makes life meaningful,
- that you're really good at, or could be good at if you learn,
- that the world actually needs,
- that can also earn you a good living.

That's what is called 'ikigai'. You might dismiss your childhood dreams, but what you discover with a deliberate quest– maybe that's what will make '*samvega*' rise in your heart.

❐❐

Chapter - 4

What's The Plan For The Weekend?

My friend Vikram bought a new house. His father gave him 60 lakh rupees, which he had saved up working his whole life. Vikram had 10 lakh rupees by himself. That made a total of 70 lakhs, but he bought a house worth 1.3 crore. So, he had to take a loan of 60 lakh rupees. He already had a car loan of 16 lakh because he wanted to buy a car worth 22 lakh.

His company keeps sending him to Lucknow, Ludhiana, and Kolkata; he keeps slogging day in and day out. No regular exercise. Always eating outside. Stressed all the time. Sometimes his blood sugar is up, other times his blood pressure is high. Once, he even had to get his gallbladder removed. He had another issue that led to his eyesight getting worse; he had to get injections in his eyes. But he still has to keep this stressful job, because there's a huge loan on his head.

I had told him that he could have got a 3-room flat for 70 lakh rupees. He still bought a 3-room flat, but in the middle of the city, 5 kilometers away from where I suggested. The area I suggested is a new development; the whole area is wide and open; there are big parks; less traffic; it's peaceful. But he wanted a flat where the main road passed right in front of the house. There's a constant noise from the traffic. Why?

Because his wife and he wanted to live in a posh area. If he ever invited friends over, he didn't want them to say, "Bro, why do you live out in the middle of nowhere?" He bought the expensive car for the same reason– to maintain his status in the office.

He tells me that he wants to quit his job. I told him again that the price of the house has gone up now– sell it for 15–20 lakhs more than what you bought it for, get a cheaper house where I suggested, get rid of the loan, and you'll still have around 10 lakhs left with you. Start your own business with that.

I gave him an idea. There are a lot of families in Haryana villages who have big houses. Some even have an extra room upstairs. They know how to cook amazing local food. They have their own farms. But they have no idea about Airbnb, registration, eco-tourism, marketing, any of that. People in the city have money, but every weekend they just go to malls; they're always looking for something fun to do. What if the whole family could go on a picnic to a village? Eat local food; drink buttermilk and nap on a charpoy; make clay pots with your own hands; spin a charkha; take photos wearing traditional clothes; do some farm work; watch the sunset.

This would improve the village family's financial situation.

Families in the city would benefit, too. They'd get a new experience for just 2000 rupees, instead of blowing money at some fancy restaurant.

It's good for the country too, if the economy decentralizes. If some of the money goes into the hands of the poor instead of the rich pocketing it all, maybe the extreme wealth gap will shrink a bit.

"The country is getting ruined because you won't quit your job, bro."

"Come on, man, don't joke around."

"I'm not joking. I'm serious."

The economy is like a pyramid. The country doesn't need a small number of large businesses; it needs a large number of small businesses. That's how jobs are created. It's clear that as the business gets bigger, jobs don't increase in the same proportion. There are businesses worth billions where only a few thousand employees work. Another friend works at a company valued at 8,000 crore, but according to their own website, they have just 2,000 employees across India, UAE, and America combined.

"Bro, we haven't got a clue about our own life… how do we think about the country?" Vikram said sarcastically.

"That's exactly why I'm saying– think about your own life first. Then you might be able to care about the country too."

"Yeah, but it doesn't work like that. Big companies have

crores to spend on marketing."

"Yeah, but those are big companies. They use a top-to-bottom approach; they start big from the get-go. You must start at ground level. As demand grows, scale your business up. That's how so many businesses have grown from small to big."

He paused, trying to find a new problem. "But how much could a village family even earn from this? And how much would I make?"

"Give them 70% of the profits and keep 30% for yourself. Find 10 such families."

Let's do the math.

One family can host three families a day.

So, 3 x 2 = 6 families on Saturday and Sunday.

In a month, that makes 6 x 4 = 24 families.

Subtract the 800 rupees cost from the 2000 fees. That makes for 1200 rupees worth of profit.

Monthly profit = 1200 x 24 = ₹ 28,800.

70% of that is ₹ 20,160– enough to keep the village family happy.

Vikram's 30% = ₹ 8,640.

If he ropes in 10 families, that's 86,400 rupees for him. As he expands the business and ropes in 100 families, that becomes ₹ 8,64,000 per month.

Now he says - no, it's not possible to save 1200 from 2000; one could barely save 500 rupees there. So, according to him, the cost of giving one family home-cooked food and tea once or twice would be 1,500 rupees. I told him that look, these families cook two meals for themselves anyway. So do they spend 1,500 x 2 x 30 = 90,000 rupees a month on their own food? There might be 2-3 extra items being made, but how could it add up to 1,500 every time?

It's like Ghalib said, "How can an agreement be reached when one doesn't wish to?" He was ready with 70 objections. He said, nowadays there are a bunch of resorts even in Haryana - like Pratapgarh Farms. All of this happens there, plus camel rides and God knows what else. So why would anyone go to someone's house? I explained, if a family of four goes to those destinations, it costs about 5,500, but here it'd be about 2,000. At those places, there's nothing exclusive. There are hundreds of people there. Here, there'd only be 1-2 families. Those picnic destinations feel like a showcase. Here, the experience would be authentic.

Some people probably prefer those resort-style places anyway; they don't care about money, love the crowd, and get better photos for Instagram. But a lot of people are looking for a raw experience, want peace, and if it's cheaper, they'll go more often. So this is a different model, and it's not fundamentally flawed.

Now he says, "You cannot do business just like that."

"So how does one do it? You have to do two years of

penance standing on one leg first?"

"You don't get it, man. Business is penance itself. So many people's businesses fail."

He's already worried about failing before even starting. What can you say to that? Still, I said, look, lots of people's businesses work as well. Why only look at the ones that fail?

This was a year ago. Now I see that some people have already started models like this and are running ads on Instagram. The people who visit there post about it, and that gives them more promotion.

Anyway, I said, if you're getting cold feet about doing something different, open a cafe nearby. Cold coffee costs 30 rupees to make and sells for 150. That's a pretty good margin.

He said, where will the money come from to start that? I explained: just rent a shop, get some kitchen stuff, spend on decoration. It'll cost 2-3 lakhs. But nope, he refused, saying that cafe culture is dead these days.

Third idea: Start a salon.

"Where will I find staff who can do good haircuts, shave, hair coloring and all that?"

"Next time you go for a haircut, talk to your barber. He'll help you find a couple of guys from his village. They know each other. Just give your barber a commission."

"No, man, I've seen that when it comes to salons, people stick to the one they've been going to for years. It's super hard to get new customers for a new salon."

I said, you've been working in marketing for years now; I'm sure you could make some use of your experience. Okay, forget it, just open a grocery store. Find a place where there's no grocery shop nearby and start there. You don't even need marketing for that. People buy from whichever is closest; the stuff is the same anyway.

"Oh, come on! After all this education, should I open a salon or a grocery store? Sit at a cash counter?"

I gave him a solid business idea, and he freaked out. And he is too embarrassed to open a salon or a store. He feels shy at the idea of running a shop, but what's he doing right now? He's just a tiny cog in a big shop. He just gave it a fancy title– Regional Sales Manager– so now it's somehow a high status job?

"Fine, if you don't want to run a shop, then just start a business, bro. If you don't like these ideas, we'll think of something else."

He said, "Markets are down across the country these days. Every business is slow. New businesses can't even be started right now." What can you even say to that? The simple truth is, he just doesn't want to do it. But why?

In the movie 'Taxi Driver,' the taxi driver 'Wizard' says something incredible to the lead character, Travis:

"You know, a man takes a job. And that job becomes what he is. You know, like– you do a thing and that's what you are. I mean, like I've been a cabbie for 17 years. 10 years at night. I still don't own my own cab. You know why? Because I don't want to. That must be what I want– to be on the night shift drivin' somebody else's cab. You understand? … you get a job, you become that job."

The guy driving a taxi becomes a taxi driver. The guy in a government job becomes a government employee. He isn't going to watch the FIFA World Cup; his FIFA is D.A., H.R.A., and grade pay. The corporate guy knows all about Arsenal, Chelsea, follows the stock market, goes to Barbeque Nation. He'll work 17 years for a company, but never have his own company after that. Even in an MBA, they only teach you how to work in a job. That's why MBAs are so specialized– HR, Marketing, Finance. Just work in that department. No one's teaching him how to start or run a business. His work experience in his job is also limited to one department. You don't learn how to do business from this work experience– neither the skill nor the mental frame.

I once asked a gutter cleaner why he chewed gutkha. He said, "We're surrounded by so much stench, our bodies ache– how else are we supposed to get by without gutkha?" After that, I didn't say anything.

A corporate worker is tied down like an ox at a mill for five days straight. Where is he going to find time to read a novel on the weekend? Why would he watch a deep, meaningful film? Why would he dig deep into his own life? His mind has already been burdened for five days straight. On weekends, he wants a beer– sometimes in a bar in his city, sometimes in a hotel room up in the hills nearby. He wants good food. He wants to sleep for a long time. During those five days, he doesn't get any special praise; so on weekends, he wants someone to compliment his clothes, shoes, phone, or car– just so he gets a bit of attention.

There are some people who do have passion, but their jobs drain it from them. They don't realize they need to preserve their passion. They're not alert to the fact that they have to protect themselves. And eventually, they become just a part of the machine.

Someone who's been grinding away like a cog from Monday to Friday wants to relax on the weekend; in that way, the five days of work shape how his weekends look. But the thing to notice is that how he spends his weekend could end up deciding how those five working days go.

He doesn't have much control over his job; he can't really do anything the way he wants during those five days. He can't do anything different. So the weekend is the only time left to do something different; change has to start from the weekend.

Some people, when the weekend comes, quietly start

gathering stuff for their farewell from the office. First, they get rid of their liabilities; they pay off loans. Then they learn a new skill. They pick up some freelance work based on that skill. And in a while, that work grows enough that they can quit their job. Or maybe they try out their stand-up comedy set at an open mic. They start their own educational YouTube channel. They upload their songs to Instagram. They draft a blueprint for a business. Name of their company, logo, tagline, website - all set. They get an app designed. They start using part of their salary to pay someone else; that is, they even start hiring for their own gig. They begin hunting for funding.

There are people whose passions can't make money immediately; it'll take time. So they start building a source of income that doesn't chew up their time and mental energy like a job does. The money won't match their salary, but it'll take less time and give them less mental stress. That way, they can pursue their passion on the side.

But on weekends, only those with *samvega*– the real drive– will put in the extra work. That restlessness, that hunger- only some people have it. Many don't. They can find it, though by breaking their own traps, by asking themselves questions. Asking 'why'. Why am I doing what I'm doing? What do I want? If money wasn't an issue, what would I want to do? What's holding me back? What am I good at? What do I want to learn? Would doing that work actually make me happy? How would money come in from that? One question after another.

Along with questioning, you've got to increase your exposure. Like we discussed, you have to experience lots of things; you have to allow yourself to be touched by deeper stuff.

Chapter - 5

The Eradication of Human Essence

Right now, this might sound simple to you - like, yeah, obviously, some drive is necessary. But in real life, most people don't even realize it. Take Vikram, for example. He has a restlessness, but it's a restlessness born out of pain and frustration– a desperation to get out of his job. It's not that kind of passion where you're dying to do something. The only thing he discusses about quitting is how to quit, not what he'll do after quitting or how to make it happen. His entire focus remains on escaping the job he's in.

That's why, he quit his job when he picked up another one. But this new job was even worse than the last one. Maybe he'll leave this one and find yet another one, but even then, chances are that things won't get better; maybe that place will have the same toxic work culture.

Escaping a golden cage isn't easy. If someone doesn't have passion, you could tell them all the stories about Alexander, Napoleon, or Steve Jobs - it won't make a difference. Motivation is like those hair oils that claim to make your hair grow. They say there are 104 wild herbs inside. But the reality is, hair growth is all about what's inside your body. Nutrition goes in; oil only gets applied on top; it doesn't really make hair grow. Sure, if you massage your scalp with some special kind of oil, it stimulates your scalp, maybe increases blood flow, and gives a tiny bit of help. But mostly, it's an internal process.

Motivation works the same way; it's got limited impact. If there's no passion inside, all the outside pumping up won't do anything. Even if you manage to hype yourself up enough to quit your job, you might just be setting yourself up for trouble. Because everything else remains the same– your entire mindset, all your systems.

Let's say I gave someone motivation– "Yeah, quit your job, filmmaking is awesome!" And then it doesn't work out for them. They start feeling blank, start missing burgers and cola, parties, nice cars. They get nervous when someone asks, "How's your new thing going?" They get stressed, regret their decision. Their family would blame me– "Our son had a decent job, you brainwashed him!" That's why I don't give out motivational speeches.

The kind of motivation that comes from within– that's your true passion, your *samvega.* You feel like doing something. For the money? No. You enjoy it, and if you get money too, that's great, but mainly because you like doing it.

People who haven't ever felt this won't get it. They're the types who brag, "I don't even have to work much." They talk about passive income; let money just flow in without doing anything. Capitalism does create those opportunities, where money makes more money for you. These days, people have a new target– get rich quick, retire at 45. If you told these people, "Drop everything, here's a lump sum equal to your lifetime salary; now do whatever you want," they wouldn't do anything. Because, well, they've got the money now. That's why people laugh at the idea of communism. They say:

"If people are only given as much as they need, why would anyone work? The only motivation humans have is money– the more you pay, the harder they'll work. Why would anyone care about work otherwise? What sense does it make to give everyone basic facilities for free? Wouldn't that just make poor people lazy?"

By the way, Karl Marx is one of the top three economists in the world. Adam Smith, Karl Marx, and John Maynard Keynes are the three pillars of economics, but according to these people, Marx was so naive that he wrote thousands of pages without ever figuring out this basic question.

In Marx's time, you could see capitalism's ugliest side. Factory workers lived in shacks near the factories. The burning coal would release so much smoke that sometimes the sun wouldn't be visible for days at a time. That led to a wave of rickets due to vitamin D deficiency. There was only one hand pump in the slum, from which dirty water came out; so outbreaks of cholera were common. The machines were dangerous; workers used to lose their hands while working. If someone became handicapped or died, there was no compensation. Children, just 10- or

12-year-olds, were put in coal mines because they were small enough to fit. The workers did all the work, but their lives were hell. The capitalists lived the good life– invest money, make money, keep making money.

Could any ordinary worker shake the whole system? No. Even when you talk about cleaning up polluted air, you're still breathing that same air. It's not hypocrisy. You can't just say, "How can you call the very air you breathe bad?" You've still got to breathe; you've still got to live. The workers had no means of production. They had to work these lousy jobs, and those jobs were limited. Capitalism's main goal is maximum profit for the capitalist, and profits are highest if you employ as few people as possible. The more machines can replace workers, the better. The invention of the steam engine led to industrialization. Big machines came in, with each machine doing work previously handled by fifty workers. Then machines got even more complex, more efficient. The scope for employment just kept shrinking.

When jobs are limited, there is auctioning of labour– people bid on who'll work for the least money. There's a constant fear: "What if I end up unemployed?" You take whatever money you can get. Workers end up competing with each other. They become selfish. If your only choices are to be a part of the oppressing class or to be oppressed, then everyone wants to climb up the pyramid. I have money today, but what about tomorrow? So, keep earning more. Healthcare is crazy expensive. If someone in my family gets sick, then what? Earn even more. My kids will only get good jobs if they go to the best schools and colleges. Maybe an MBBS course will cost a crore rupees. Keep earning.

If you can't get a corporate job, be a top official. Be a politician. Make money from there. If I'm taking bribes, aren't others doing the same? If I've got the chance to take a bribe, why not? If a hospital offers a commission for an unnecessary heart surgery, why not? That's how things work. No one really cares for others; everyone's out for themselves. Times aren't good for doing good deeds. Make money. Move up. Hustle.

Marx understood that people are living in such an atmosphere of selfishness and greed; how would they accept the teachings of Jesus Christ? Yes, the very definition of communism comes from the Bible. Jesus says somewhere–

"From each according to his ability, to each according to his need."

If someone is young and strong, he should work more. If someone is disabled, old, or a pregnant woman, less work could be done– according to their ability.

If someone's hungrier, let them eat more. If they're not so hungry, eat less– according to need.

Even in Hinduism, it's said that all land belongs to Gopal. Gandhi ji also talked about this, saying that whoever takes more than they need is actually stealing. In Islam, 'zakaat' is one of the five pillars, which means giving charity. In Sikhism, 'dasvandh' also refers to donation. Jainism talks about 'aparigraha', which refers to non-possessiveness.

But because of the brutal form of capitalism that existed, people were anxious and scared. That anxiety led to selfishness and greed. Would such scared, selfish, and greedy people accept this message from religion– that your contribution should be according to your ability, and you should get according to your needs? Nope, they'd say this is nonsense. Where's the motivation to work in that? Such an objection makes perfect sense within that web of capitalism.

Karl Marx introduced the concept of 'dominant ideology' way back in 1845, when he was 27 years old, with Friedrich Engels in their book The German Ideology. There, they state that the ideas of the ruling class are the ruling ideas of society. Basically, the class that dominates society ends up setting the ideas in everyone's minds.

Where there's capitalism, there's bound to be consumerism, because that's the fuel for capitalism. People will consume more; there will be a race to collect stuff, competition to earn more; but the priority in that system isn't jobs for everyone. So there will be auctioning of labour, selfishness, greed, jealousy. Work is organized so that the capitalist's costs are kept low and profits are high, not so that workers enjoy their work.

A long time ago, when an artisan worked by hand, they'd make the whole product themselves– chairs, pots, shoes, clothes, mats, statues, sweets. They'd take pride in what they created themselves. They'd actually use their own products too. They'd get instant feedback from people, try to improve themselves, work from home, maybe hum a tune as they did their craft, with their family around. And even the kids would learn by watching or helping out. After lunch, maybe take a nap. If you felt like taking a day off, you just would. Work was there, but there was no stress around the work. Work filled life with meaning. The skill was a part of your personality, your identity. Work and family went hand in hand. And the wider community was important too– religious functions, festivals.

So firstly, humans used to create; there was creativity in work. Secondly, humans were social creatures.

Karl Marx said that capitalism causes the 'alienation of man'– it alienates him, distances him from his humanity, takes away what is unique to the human species.

All other animals only do what's needed for survival. But humans, while considering themselves as subjects, view what they create as objects. Other animals are influenced by their surroundings, but there's no conscious intent in what they do. Humans, on the other hand, think.

They're interested in many activities, which let them connect with society, help mutual survival, and also make them feel good mentally.

Within their historical conditions, humans have preferences, imagination. They ask questions– like "why?"– and that's how they give purpose to their lives.

But in capitalist society, you have to run according to what others expect from you. You're stuck choosing among whatever jobs are available, whatever you can get. If you have to work on weekends, so be it. There's no real choice in it.

The products you make– you didn't design them. The interesting thing is, even the customer didn't really design them. It's the capitalist who decides the design, based on mass production, minimizing cost and maximizing profit.

Capitalism doesn't just alienate you from your product, but also from the process of production. Now you don't make the entire thing; you're just a small part of a huge system. This is shown as slapstick humor in Charlie Chaplin's movie Modern Times, where the worker is trapped in the machines, and his hands just keep repeating the same motion. He doesn't even know much about the product.

During my visit to Ranbaxy's plant, I saw how medicines are made, but you can just watch that stuff on YouTube too. So if a worker is in HR or accounts, they won't know anything; but even if they're in production, they still won't have a full grasp of the product. Sure, medicines are technical products; no one expects a worker to know all the scientific details.

But take cars. I did my internship at Sona Koyo Steering Systems, which makes steering systems for several car companies. Another company makes tyres for the car companies. Then somewhere, the car is assembled.

Think about cell phones; components are made in one place, assembled in another, marketed somewhere else.

Still, cars and cell phones are complex products. Now think about bread. Watch a video of a big bakery on YouTube. Workers don't decide the recipe. That's all set and standardized by the company.

Even in the process itself, there's not much for the worker:

- Someone pours flour into the mixing machine.
- Someone puts a big tub under the machine to catch the dough.
- Then it's taken to another machine, where it's cut into little chunks shaped like bread.
- Someone puts those into small molds and sets them on a shelf to ferment.
- After a little while, someone pulls out the molds, presses the fermented dough, puts a cut in it if it's sourdough bread, and pops it in the oven.
- Someone takes the baked bread out of the oven.

Even if one worker did all of this, their hands aren't really involved anywhere– they're just putting pieces from machine to machine. If they quit and someone else takes over, nothing about the bread would change.

Look at a bigger factory; the machines are enormous and do all the work from start to finish, and the bread comes out packed, with a worker only visible at the very beginning.

Ask that worker to make bread at home. It's not a given that they can. Because here, they're not making bread; they're just operating the bread-making machine. The artisan who once dreamed of becoming the best baker in town– that just doesn't exist anymore.

They're now far from their purpose, their conscious decisions, their product, the production process, their creativity. Even the workers they're around– they aren't collaborators anymore; now they're in competition. They've moved away from home, parents, spouse, kids. Even if they live at home, they leave in the morning when the kids are still asleep and come back when the kids are asleep again. They're alone, empty, no pride in their work, no purpose. Why would anyone want to do this kind of job without the motivation of money? Why would they accept "from each according to their ability, to each according to their need"?

Marx absolutely understood this, and that's why he talked about a middle stage. He even debated this with Mikhail Bakunin, who wanted society to go stateless directly. Marx argued that to avoid shocking people, there needed to be socialism first, as a transition from capitalism to communism, where you'd get according to your contribution and contribute according to your ability. The only people who'd have an issue with that would be the bourgeoisie, who owned factories with their money and claimed all the profits.

Marx said that the means of production should be in the hands of the vanguard party of revolutionaries. They'd plan production. Workers wouldn't have a problem, since they were earning so little before– factory owners auctioned off their labour– so this would be better. There would be no competition, jobs for all, basic amenities for everyone, no reason for fear or greed. In that atmosphere, people would gradually become better; everything would get streamlined, and over time, the state itself would wither away. And then the beautiful dream of communism would be real, where there's no rich or poor, no discrimination.

Everyone would have amenities, and nobody would have private property. Everything would belong to everyone. In capitalism, the capitalist has all the free time, and the worker has none; but here, since everyone works, the work would finish quickly, and workers would finally have time for their intellectual and moral development.

Moving away from competition, anxiety, selfishness, and greed, people would do work that doesn't distance them from their humanity, that isn't boring, that gives them purpose, that makes them happy while doing it. Scientists would invent with joy, farmers would grow food, someone would make clothes, someone would make music. Marx says that work wouldn't just be a means to survive; it would, like food, clothing, shelter, and education, be a fundamental human need.

It all sounds very appealing. But it's obvious that the world's never been able to turn that dream into reality;

what we saw in the name of communism was actually dictatorship and oppression. In the Soviet Union, Stalin started the 'nepreryvka' policy, which meant continuous work. The work used to be in shifts. So the husband's day off, the wife's day off, and the child's school holiday would all fall on different days. In the official newspaper Pravda, a worker wrote a letter saying, what good is a holiday if I have to spend it alone? Work was just as boring as ever– the same 'alienation of man' that existed in capitalism. That's why many people called it "state capitalism." The economy crumbled due to centralization; millions were killed, millions more died because of those policies. The same kind of thing happened under Mao Zedong in China.

There was a time when, in those countries, anyone who opposed the government would be labeled anti-communist and killed. On the other side, critics in places like Argentina, Guatemala, Indonesia, Taiwan, Finland, Germany, and others were called communists and killed. It's a good thing that those times are behind us now.

Poverty was rampant in the countries of the Soviet bloc. People were so dissatisfied that they would try to escape the country by making hot-air balloons. In such a situation, the collapse of the Soviet Union was only natural.

Where did the problem begin? Actually, Karl Marx missed out on something Plato said: only those who have no attachment to power deserve it. But the paradox is that such people never try to come into power. Most people who do end up in power are the ones addicted to it, and power usually corrupts people's minds. So, it's practically impossible that the vanguard party would slowly let the state wither away and then communism– a society without any government– would arrive.

Bhagat Singh also stated that the ideal of his revolution was the reorganization of society on Marxist lines. He even chanted slogans like "Long live the socialist revolution" and "Long live Communist International" in court. He referred to capitalists as parasites who loot the labour of workers.

Let's suppose, just for a second, the vanguard party's leader is a truly selfless person, like Bhagat Singh, and they do get into power– but still, what after that person is gone? The possibility of dictatorship always remains. That's why there was never a scope for improvement in a single-party Leninist political system.

Democracy has its own flaws– like, if fools are in the majority, the chances of a fool being elected increase manyfold. But so far, we've seen that whatever its shortcomings, democracy is still the best system. It should be protected, and attempts should be made to improve it further.

Karl Marx missed out on understanding the intoxication of power, but the bigger problem is that many communists turned Marx into a god, treated his books as holy scriptures, and saw communism as if it were a religion. Just like we see people proudly calling themselves staunch Hindus or staunch Muslims, there are also staunch communists who use terms like 'reformist' as an insult, accusing others of being revisionists– i.e., amending the words of 'God' Karl Marx.

And like many Hindus and Muslims, these staunch communists haven't really read their holy books– i.e., Marx's own writings– forget interpreting them according to the present times. These kinds of fools are the Naxalites, who idolize Stalin, Mao, and his general Lin Biao; who think they'll pull off a coup in India and then the whole world. The impossibility of this makes it ridiculous, but bigger than the question of feasibility is that they're so brainwashed, they don't even want to see history. They refuse to acknowledge how brutal the rule of Stalin and Mao really was. The Leninist political system clearly turned out to be a foolish idea.

To use Karl Marx as the basis for a violent revolution is like saying Prophet Muhammad adopted violence or that in the Bhagavad Gita, Lord Krishna tells Arjun that war is the path to heaven. It's unfair to pull something out of its original context.

So, what was the context? In Marx's time, there was no democracy anywhere in the world. The revolutions of 1848 were a major event of that era. Leftists of the French Revolution had introduced the idea of nationalism, which led people to see themselves as a single unit (a nation); in many countries of Europe, people began revolting to remove the control of kings. Slavery ended in Austria and Hungary. Denmark shifted from being an absolute monarchy to becoming a constitutional monarchy. But in many countries, revolutions were crushed. Democracy was still a distant dream.

You could say there was democracy in America, but in reality, power just shifted from British capitalists to American capitalists. When gold was discovered in Georgia, the government forcibly evicted the 60,000 indigenous people who lived there. Never mind that they were deprived of the gold found on their own land; thousands of them even died of hunger and disease during the journey to their new home. That path is called the 'Trail of Tears.' In 1830, a law was passed to push them out, showing how laws were just official covers for atrocities. Black people were still slaves at that time. Slavery could only be abolished in 1865 under the leadership of Abraham Lincoln. Women and poor workers didn't have the right to vote. Even in England, where there was a so-called constitution and parliament, we've already discussed the grim state of the workers.

In this context, a violent revolution was like how Netaji Bose was fighting against British rule through violence. On the other hand, Gandhi Ji was uniting people through nonviolence– using non-cooperation and civil disobedience, refusing to pay taxes, breaking the salt law, burning over a lakh English clothes in Mumbai, and using the spinning wheel to boost Indian confidence and the Indian economy. This was also a path that turned out to be effective. So it's no surprise that communist revolutionaries like Che Guevara and Ho Chi Minh respected Gandhi Ji. Bhagat Singh also advised his father to follow Gandhi Ji.

With time, democracy came to the world. But staunch communists stuck with violent revolution. Even those communists who abandoned violence and embraced democracy weren't all that flexible either. They too began to look at Karl Marx as a god rather than a philosopher. This gets more absurd when you realize that Marx never saw himself as some messiah sent by God. Like, one critic of his book Das Kapital asked why he didn't talk in detail about the forms that socialism and communism would take. At the end of the second edition of Das Kapital, Marx himself acknowledged this and said –

"Thus the Paris Revue Positiviste reproaches me for, on the one hand, treating economics metaphysically, and, on the other hand, imagine this!– for confining myself merely to the critical analysis of the actual facts, instead of writing recipes for the cook-shops of the future."

Marx explained that the purpose behind writing Das Kapital was to discover the 'economic laws of motion' of modern society.

In the book, The German Ideology, he also said that communism is an ideal– a movement whose conditions spring from present circumstances themselves.

So even though staunch communists treat 'reformist' as a cuss word, Marx himself praised trade unions in the preface to the first volume of Das Kapital, saying that they were a major change in the existing relationship between labour and capital. When the Factory Acts came into force in England, Marx didn't reject them; he actually called them an important reform. He said that through legal means, there was now a limit on working hours, making it clear when the worker was selling his time and when his own time began.

In this way, over the past 175 years, a lot of positive changes have occurred. People who think the left has failed and Marx lost have the same understanding of history as the Naxals.

The truth is that given the hellish circumstances at that time, things kept on slowly improving from there. Today, all across the world, we see trade unions, the right to strike, laws against child labour, limits on weekly working hours, sick leave, minimum wage, maternity leave for women, employee insurance, provident fund, comfortable workplaces with air and light, fire safety norms. Many companies have even started job-rotation policies, so that every employee can understand the whole process.

All this was possible because of activists, reformists, and socialists. Some positive people in the business world played a part too, like Robert Owen or Ratan Tata.

On the other hand, there are those despicable capitalists whom Karl Marx called vampires and Bhagat Singh called parasites; they also kept spreading their hoods like snakes; robbed workers' lives of all joy, and didn't value their personal talents at all. Work stayed boring there. No creativity. The worker left no personal impression. They could be removed and replaced in an instant.

At most workplaces, the 'alienation of man' still exists. The worker is far removed from the product and the production process, far from other workers, far from their own humanity, and from their own conscious intent– why am I doing this, what's the purpose, what do I like?

Some people who work in research are robbed of their names– like, who exactly made Microsoft Windows? We don't know. Novartis's medicine Zolgensma is one of the world's most expensive drugs– 17 crore rupees for one dose. They justify it by saying that it took a lot of research, but who did the research? We don't know. The company's name devours the names of the actual people.

Now, in 2025, again it's not clear when the worker's own time actually begins. Work comes calling at any time– at the office, at home, on a Wednesday or a Sunday, day or night. Even if it's not direct work, there are always emails, phone calls, follow-ups, and the stress of office work.

Then there are jobs where you're exposed to cancer-causing particles in the air or chemicals that can damage your lungs.

And the work pressure– where does one even begin! Someone said that you have to work 70 hours a week, and then someone said 90 hours a week. They tell you, "This is your target, this is your deadline." Who sets these targets?

God didn't create these deadlines; they're all made up by the companies. They say they have flexible work timings, but it never means you can sign off early on your kid's birthday; flexible work timings just means that you're on the job day or night. They won't directly tell you to work nights, but the company targets and deadlines are such that, to meet them, you'll have to always be at work.

Noam Chomsky once commented on how corporations are controlled top-down:

You can be inserted in the middle somewhere, like a junior manager, take orders from the top, and hand them down below. At the very bottom, people are allowed to rent themselves to it; it's called getting a job."

The solution could be doubling the number of workers, but that would mean that those stingy capitalists have to pay more people. So instead, make the workers compete among themselves. Turn a part of the salary into incentives, so that the worker keeps working in the name of ambition and career growth, like an ox yoked to a plough.

If someone speaks out against this toxic work culture or demands laws to address it, they're quickly labelled as lazy, a slacker, a loser, anti-development, and what not. Let them say what they want; let people rant if they have to. You just focus on claiming your own freedom.

Constantly adjusting has led us straight to 'karoshi'. Never heard of karoshi? It's a Japanese term that means death from overwork. A worker might have money, but still suffers from malnutrition; no restful sleep; no family life; no decent system for three meals; exercise is a distant dream. There's so much physical pressure and mental stress on top of that that it leads to death from a heart attack or stroke.

If someone dies by suicide under such circumstances, it's called 'karojisatsu'. There's a forest about a two-hour drive from Tokyo, Aokigahara, which literally means "blue trees meadow," but it's notorious as the suicide forest. Some people crack under the stress of being fired, others under the pressure of just continuing at work.

And this isn't just about Japan. In many countries like Sweden, the USA, China, South Korea, and India, we're seeing deaths caused by work overload. The official website of the US Occupational Safety and Health Administration reports that 120,000 deaths per year in America can be traced back to workplace stress. A joint report from the World Health Organization (WHO) and the International Labour Organization (ILO) in 2021 stated that, in 2016, 1.9 million people worldwide died due to work-related causes. Out of those, 350,000 died of heart disease, 400,000 from stroke, 450,000 due to workplace air pollution, and 750,000 from long working hours.

And those who don't die– you'll see that many of them have become pretty much like zombies. No dreams, no enthusiasm. Permanent fatigue has taken them hostage. Loneliness eats away at them from inside. Just last year, WHO declared loneliness a "global public health concern."

It reminds me of that poem by Jigar Moradabadi, where he says that life is slowly being devoid of life itself.

So what now? How's this supposed to work? The corporate culture has its own strange ways of coping. Reducing work pressure to kill stress isn't on their agenda; instead, they teach you how to manage stress. The HR department will have people make rangoli during Diwali, and arrange team-building exercises. At times, there is an office trip for employees with facilities for their consumption; they could do photo ops and get attention on Instagram. You can do the same at your local mall on weekends.

They'll even teach you meditation. Someone once asked Osho if one should meditate for 10 minutes every morning. He said– why just ten minutes, why not the whole day? Is half an hour of breathing in the morning enough to get by? He argued, why not have your whole day in meditation?

In another lecture, he said that meditation isn't about getting away from life or action; it doesn't mean escaping. It just shows you a new path, where you become the calm center of a storm. Your life keeps moving, now with even more intensity; more joy, more clarity, vision, and creativity, and you watch it all unfold in a state of peace.

But your company's HR will never talk about that kind of meditation. They're not talking about joy or creativity. All they'll say is, just close your eyes for 15 minutes in the morning and focus on your breath; it'll calm your overactive mind just enough so that the company can grind you all over again. Voila– stress managed!

Karl Marx actually had a similar thought when he called religion the opium of the masses. He said –

"Religion is the sigh of the oppressed creature, the heart of a heartless world, and the soul of soulless conditions. It is the opium of the people."

Marx criticized religion because, for him, the state and society create religion. It's an inverted consciousness of an inverted world. It is the imaginary realization of the human essence since the human essence has not acquired any true reality. The struggle against religion is, therefore, indirectly the struggle against that world whose spiritual aroma is religion.

Modern company meditation is just the same thing. If that's not enough, there's always psychotherapy. Therapy itself isn't wrong; what's wrong is needing therapy because work is making people miserable instead of happy. We're just accepting that the problem is here to stay; all that's changing is that the pills are getting passed around. All sorts of stuff to numb yourself is on offer– pizza, cola, cars, pools, social status, Instagram likes, religion, meditation, therapy, video games. Just play a game on your phone on the train ride home from the office, kill some more time.

Feeling lonely? Japan's got solutions for that too. You can rent parents for a day. You can also rent a girlfriend or boyfriend to act out a relationship and make you feel good. You can even hire someone to just sit with you for a while and drink coffee together.

Do you feel like your emotions have dried up inside? There's a fix for that too. It's called 'rui-katsu', which literally means the search for tears. People gather in a room and a professional tells them an emotional story to make them cry. They show you emotional short films. Folks gather, and everyone cries together. Like therapy, there's nothing wrong with rui-katsu in itself. If that's the only way out, it's good that at least there is something. But the real question is– why do things have to reach a point where people's emotions are dried up inside?

All this paraphernalia is at your disposal. But the central aspect of your life– your job, the thing you spend the most time on– is utter nonsense. It's like being at a music concert with thousands of people; the chairs are comfy, the decor is stunning, there are massive lights, colorful balloons, smoke machines, giant screens, an enormous stage, amazing graphics at the back, background dancers– but the singer's voice is downright terrible, off-key, scratchy. It'd feel weird, right? Especially if you've heard what real music sounds like. But if nobody else seems to find it weird, if everyone's busy "enjoying" the concert, you'll end up pretending to enjoy it too.

Herd mentality is a powerful force. On top of that, there's cultural hegemony; culture keeps stamping approval on this whole mess. You'll tell yourself that this is how things are. The rich and their wealth will be glorified. You'll be told you should aspire to be just like them. Inside this trap, that's what success looks like. Those already in the trap–they want you to stay trapped as well. But can you break out of it? Can you even see that it is a trap?

□□

Chapter - 6

The Matrix of Collective Greed

Imagine there's a jail with fifty prisoners. There is a race among them. Only 45 people participate in the race. The 5 who don't participate, face mockery. They are criticized and told that trying is what's important; participating in the race is a bigger thing than winning or losing. But these 5 people do not take part.

The remaining 45 prisoners run. Only one will win the race, but all 45 are under the illusion that they can win. Eventually, one person wins. What does he get as a prize? Does he get freedom from jail? No. The freedom is given to those 5 who were trying to find a way out of jail.

The race winner gets a medal, and others' eyes are on that medal. The other 44 are clapping for him. That's what he tried for. People ask him how one could become like him. He says he doesn't want to be like himself; why would anyone else want to be like him?

Elon Musk said this in an interview. His two marriages broke down. His girlfriend wasn't satisfied with his money either. His daughter said that she doesn't want any relationship with her father. Elon Musk has also been depressed. He shared this on Twitter. A Silicon Valley investor, Chris Sacca, who knows him personally, said Musk has no true friends - people who can tell him the truth to his face and keep him grounded. If you don't worship Musk, you could easily see from Elon Musk's Twitter activity how insecure he is.

Look at how many rich and popular celebrities like Honey Singh, Deepika Padukone, and Kapil Sharma have all been depressed. Hollywood star Jim Carrey also said:

> "I think everyone should get rich and famous and do everything they ever dreamed of so they can see that it's not the answer."

So, what's the point of a race that takes you to a destination where there's no joy?

But motivational gurus ignore this and keep saying, "You too can become Elon Musk." The media also continues to worship these idols. Magazines show you lists of the world's top 20 richest people. What's the use of knowing that? Still, since people want to know, magazines tell them. And since magazines tell, that's why people get interested.

The reel of Mukesh Ambani's son's wedding fills your feed. The cost of someone's watch, how expensive was someone's necklace - all of this gets fed to you. Songs and movies show the same. Hotels, swimming pools, big cars. No matter what the winners say, 44 prisoners still want to win the race. That's their aspiration. That's why the system runs.

If people stop being amazed by luxury cars worth crores, then why would those cars sell? Why would anyone buy a diamond necklace worth crores if wearing it wouldn't get them attention? Craving for this ego-boost is the secret of this consumerist system's energy.

Whenever this attention is received, it feels good, and the rest of the time, the heart remains sad and craves that same attention. In this way, a person becomes a puppet of others. Yes, wealth disparity exists in the world, but the inequality of attention is also huge. On one side are those who are completely alone. No one listens to them. On the other side are celebrities, who get so much attention that it becomes too hard to handle, because there are only 24 hours in a day. When millions of fans come into the picture, time with family and friends decreases. You have to attend so many parties, and do fan management.

When praise from the world comes, it's great; but when criticism arrives, the scale of that criticism is equally huge. If you lose an election, your film flops, you're removed from the CEO position, or someone says something wrong about you, then your spectacle becomes global–memes, jokes, ridicule. The ego that was boosted by attention now suffers a heavy blow, and stress sets in.

First, climbing the pyramid takes effort, then staying there takes effort, but even the enjoyment isn't the same anymore. People feel duped. They get sidelined. The race keeps going on. The movie "Fashion" showed this well.

It was said to be a movie about fashion and modeling, but the system of the whole world is the same. There's always a showstopper. Then someone else comes in as the new supermodel. Fashion shows are bigger than any model. Jail is much bigger than any race-winning prisoner.

If we go towards freedom, there's no encouragement from jail. You'll be called stupid: "He had a decent job, left it, what a fool!" Osho says–

"No society wants you to become wise. It's against every society's investment. If people are wise, they can't be exploited. If they're clever, they can't be kept in slavery. They can't be forced to live like robots, a mechanical life. Their personality will come out. There will be a sweet smell of rebellion around them. They'll want to live in freedom. Freedom comes with intelligence, and no society wants you to be free. It becomes a threat to those in power, a threat to systems of oppression."

That's why from childhood, your training is of the same kind. You are trained to fit into that system. Renowned astronomer Carl Sagan, in an interview, explained how the educational system kills curiosity in children–

"My experience is that whether you talk to kindergarten kids or first graders, you find a class full of children interested in science. They ask deep questions– what is a dream, why do we have thumbs, why is the moon round, when is the world's birthday, why is grass green? These are important, profound questions. They come out like bubbles from inside children. Then you talk to twelfth graders. Nothing like that happens. They've lost curiosity. Something very wrong has happened between kindergarten and twelfth grade."

The interviewer says that if in twelfth grade you're interested in science, you'll be called a nerd. Carl Sagan agrees.

Where does that curiosity go? It gets lost in completing the syllabus and getting marks. The system is designed to reward those who walk the trodden path. Whether it's America or India, the rote-learning system is still a terrible truth of education. You just need good marks to move to the next class. It's not that the conceptual clarity won't get you marks; but even if you don't have clarity, you will still get marks. All you have to do is submit assignments.

Noam Chomsky says that if a child says he won't do a stupid assignment, that he finds it pointless, he won't get marks. The one who quietly submits the assignment will move to the next class. This is how the education system selects based on obedience.

It is shown that only some people are leaders. The attempt to develop leadership skills in everyone doesn't happen. If that happened, everyone in every neighborhood would start protesting about bad roads. Everyone would start making their own decisions. Without mental slavery, how will this system work where people are made to work boring 16-hour shifts? Your training from home and school is all about following instructions. You're told what to do all the time. Discipline is promoted as a great virtue.

All of this may sound like some conspiracy theory. Is everyone scheming together to make you a mental slave? Is the world like the movie The Truman Show? But if it's happening to everyone, then who's doing it? Do all politicians and capitalists have secret meetings? Are they the jailers of that prison, making all the prisoners race?

The jailers are those same people, but the race is organized by the jail– i.e., the collective consciousness of the jail. That collective consciousness is created based on the material conditions of the prison. If you run in the race, you get to consume more and receive more attention.

The desire to win that race also fuels filmmakers - they too want a 100-crore film. So they won't make movies that make you think, rather they make movies that appease people's existing mindset. People love violence, so show violence; glorify weapons; make crime entertaining.

If someone says the film is misogynist and filled with toxic masculinity, then ignore it or make excuses that movies don't matter. Distributors and producers want the same kind of movies because the producer is a businessman; he's also in the race to make money. An actor is racing to become a superstar. The lyricist doesn't care if the song they're writing for a film sends a bad message to society. The singer wants 100 million views, and he will get views by putting a stamp of approval on wrong attitudes and aspirations of people. Look at the Punjabi songs - how many songs about guns and weapons have been made by now? And that's the trend now in Haryana as well.

The company making bread won't benefit from connecting the worker to his humanity. Their production is higher when workers are used as cogs of a machine.

People want jobs with higher packages. They'll get that from working for big companies. Those big companies will recruit from top MBA colleges. You get admitted to those top colleges by taking coaching from top coaching institutes. Parents spend a fortune on coaching. College fees run in lakhs. Loans are taken for that. Once the loan is on your head, starting a business after getting an MBA makes no sense; you'll have to first get a job. MBA anyways doesn't prepare anyone to start a business; it prepares them to get a job.

After paying off the student loan, if you start a business, is there true freedom? No, the race continues because even businesspeople are not free from stress. Not every business owner enjoys what he does. They don't start their business thinking about what the world truly needs or where joy lies. They're just thinking about how to make more money. They will make good money selling momos made with maida, deep-fried in refined oil and coated with mayonnaise because that's what's trending now.

During an MBA, you are taught the same thing in Business Analysis. The popular model called SWOT analysis involves looking at strengths, weaknesses, opportunities, and threats. It's not meant to figure out if the product is really needed by the world or not. It's said that if there's no demand, then demand can be created. It's also not about assessing how ecologically sustainable the product is.

Coca-Cola was earlier being sold in glass bottles as well, but the hassle of returning bottles was a concern, as it increased the cost for the company. One solution could have been decentralizing the production, which would also create more jobs. There would be less need to add preservatives in food and drinks. But again, it would increase the costs of the company. So, to hell with ecological sustainability! Every minute, millions of plastic bottles are made and sold.

What is the whole marketing MBA course about? It's about understanding what cognitive biases humans have and then exploiting them; manipulating people this way. For example:

- There's a popular business case study where a toothpaste company's sales were declining; someone suggested increasing the diameter of the toothpaste tube slightly, so that people wouldn't notice, leading them to unknowingly use more toothpaste. After some time, the sales increased. Wow, applause!

- Another case study: 30 years ago, American Airlines wanted to boost profits. So a manager suggested removing one olive from every passenger's salad; nobody would notice. The company saved $40,000 a year. Wow, applause!
- Decoy pricing is another such strategy that plays directly on uninformed people's minds.

  (i) A burger costs 50 rupees,

  (ii) burger + cola costs 100 rupees,

  (iii) burger, cola, and fries combo costs 110 rupees.

The second option is actually a decoy– an irrelevant choice just to trap the customer. Nobody really buys that. The options the company is serious about are the first and the third one. The company wants more customers to pick the third, but when people compare the first and third option, the latter seems expensive.

To make the third one look valuable, they insert the decoy. So now so the customer compares again -

(i) burger + cola costs 100 rupees,

(iii) burger, cola, and fries combo costs 110 rupees.

He thinks, "Hey, only 10 more rupees for fries with the third option." This way, more combo packs can be sold. Wow, applause!

There are countless such marketing tricks and branding strategies based on the study of human behavior. There's nothing wrong with understanding human nature and using it. But the question is: what are you using it for?

I watch Oliver Sjostrom's workout videos on YouTube while exercising. There's a percentage bar at the bottom of the screen showing how much of the workout is done. I noticed it gives me a little push– now I've done 35%, now 65%, now 90%, only 10% left. This human behavior has been shown in many studies: tracking progress step by step helps people reach their goals. Oliver used this to motivate people to finish their workouts.

So, whether it's a job or a business, it's possible that you're just part of the same prison and running in that same race for money. Freelancers can be caught in the same trap. A freelance editor doesn't care why their editing is used. Whether it fosters superstition in society or strengthens a scientific perspective isn't their concern. They just see how much money they're earning. They can easily brush it off, saying, "I'm just an editor."

A female actor was seen acting in campaign videos for three different political parties at different times. She has no ideology; she doesn't care why her acting is used.

She's still just an actor in the political campaign videos; even the politician himself doesn't care about ideology. Whichever party gives him a ticket, wherever victory is likely, he'll take that ticket. The system is such that tickets are bought; if he spends money on a ticket, he's going to recover it. The five-year salary of an MLA or MP isn't as much as what they spend on buying a ticket and their campaign.

The party chief surely has the option to decide whom to give tickets to and whom to deny, but they are also caught in the race for money and power. If a candidate has good chances of winning, then this would increase his party's seats in the assembly. Thus, he'll have a higher chance of becoming Chief Minister or Prime Minister. Then they'll play money games with big companies– taking campaign funds from them and giving them business in return. If asked, they'll act helpless, saying, "People don't vote based on honesty; they vote on free booze, chicken, blankets." That's why they have to take election funds from wealthy sponsors.

Everyone says, why should only they shoulder all the social responsibility. If every part is broken, the whole system made from those parts will be broken too. Everyone's troubled by corruption, by the race for money, but not by their own behavior, rather by others' attitudes.

Someone complains about their doctor not listening to their illness properly even for five minutes and quickly handing out a bunch of pills. Some tenant has occupied the doctor's flat, and the doctor is upset with the lawyer and judge because his case keeps getting deferred. The lawyer is angry at the electrician who didn't do a proper job at his house. Two weeks later, the AC breaks again; when they call him, he won't pick up. The electrician is annoyed because the school teachers aren't teaching his kids properly. The teacher is upset because a singer's vulgar song is corrupting his child. The singer is upset because instead of paying him, the music company is extorting money from him in the name of promoting him. The music company is upset because CDs and cassettes have gone out of fashion; earlier, people bought cassette CDs of ghazals or listened to pop music, but now what you need is YouTube views. The model where people pay 10 rupees to download a song doesn't work because there are already so many songs on YouTube. The owner of the music company is troubled by this new system. Besides this, he is upset with the restaurants that, despite everything being expensive, the service isn't good; the food isn't fresh; the paneer tastes weird. The restaurant owner is troubled by the online delivery partner, that due to the pressure of quick deliveries, they are not able to prepare fresh food; today all restaurants run on this system of frozen foods; their expenses have shot up, taxes are high, and rent in that locality is way too much. They want to get their child admitted to MBBS, where the fees amount to a crore. The one who started the medical college is troubled by government regulations. A politician is demanding bribes from him. The politician is scared that he might lose the next election.

So, does the buck stop at the politician? Does the capitalist have the final say? Well, it's true that compared to others, these jailers have some extra power, but it's not entirely in their control either. As we said earlier, it is hard for an honest politician to win the election if they don't have campaign funds. Similarly, some companies are at risk due to the increasing monopoly of a few big ones. The big company has given big discounts and lowered its prices so much that the small company is losing its customers.

The rich businessman owning the biggest company can probably move things around a bit, but why would he? Is he some incarnation of Buddha? Had he been so, he wouldn't have been the richest guy. You respect him because he has earned so much money. You also want to earn money like him. That's how this system keeps running.

You say, "What difference would it make if it's just me who changes? Everyone else is doing wrong, so why shouldn't I?" Today, money is necessary to survive. You need a lot of money for a decent life. Everything is so expensive. And without money, nobody cares about you. That's true, but everyone thinks that way. And this is how the collective soul of the prison keeps the race going. There's no special conspiracy to enslave you; you are part of that system which has enslaved you. Maintaining this prison doesn't require any special plans. Material conditions, cultural hegemony, society's collective consciousness– all of it keeps this system alive just like this.

Planning, however, is needed to break this web. From where do we break it? Who will break it? How can it be broken? Is it even possible to break this web? Do we now return to communism and a vanguard party? But that experiment has already failed.

So, is there no way to change anything? One way is this: to change your life, you don't need to wait for the world to change.

Chapter - 7

Vocal for Local

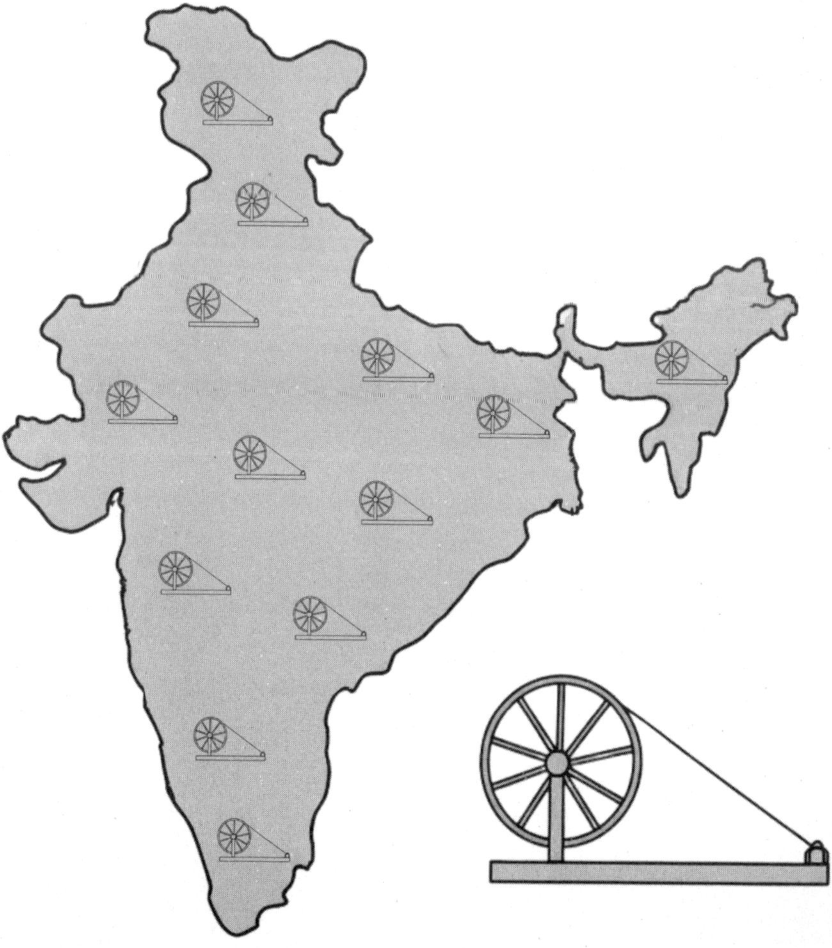

The situation is no longer such that you are either a landlord or a farm labourer. That you're either a capitalist or a worker in a factory; and if you're a labourer, then you have no surplus left, i.e. whatever you earn, it's barely enough to get by. That's not how it is anymore. Today, there's a middle class in the world.

When the wave of industrialization began, and businesses started to expand, there arose a need for accountants, managers, and secretaries. With the advent of democracy, government jobs also emerged. The middle class was formed from these people. Technically, the middle class was born in Europe, around the year of 1750. They are considered to have played a significant role in the French Revolution as well. The growth of the middle class was also helped by the production and export of silk.

Department stores were opening up in America and England. By the 1920s, consumerism was widespread, meaning that consuming goods and services beyond just one's basic needs became a goal in itself. New products were being seen in stores, with advertisements heard on the radio. These could be purchased in installments.

In 1946, the era of modern venture capital began. To enable private sector investment in businesses founded by soldiers returning from the Second World War, the American Research and Development Corporation was started.

About a hundred years before that, 28 weavers and skilled workers in England formed the world's first modern cooperative society, called the Rochdale Pioneers. These 28 people were the owners of their own trades; they worked themselves; they had a shared shop where they sold their products.

At first glance, these two models are opposites: in the cooperative model, the workers have total ownership; in the venture capital model, a person invests the money, someone else runs the business, and perhaps yet another person does the actual work. But the commonality in both models is that people who don't have much money are also able to start their own businesses. It's true that the venture capitalist earns just by virtue of their money, but the business founder also earns something and holds a share in the business.

Another model is starting a business by taking a loan. One way of doing this is the committee system, where several people contribute money together. Ten people pool in funds, one person picks the committee (i.e., takes the money), starts something with it, earns an income, and then pays back the others with interest in monthly installments. In a way, it's the stock market of the poor, where you don't buy shares but debentures; you don't have ownership in the business, but you get a predetermined rate of interest. Naturally, this system operates informally rather than being under regulations, so there's a risk of things going wrong. But the model is brilliant, if only it could be formalized.

The formal system is that banks can give you a loan under certain conditions to start your own business. Dr Muhammad Yunus– currently the Chief Advisor of Bangladesh's interim government– received the 2006 Nobel Peace Prize because he founded the Grameen Bank and introduced the concepts of microcredit and microfinance. Small loans are given to poor people– some get 10,000, others get 50,000. If a few people form a self-help group and take loans together, they can get bigger amounts, like 1,50,000. No collateral needs to be pledged. There is a disciplined plan to repay the microloan over three years. Easy repayment plans are available monthly, weekly, or even such where the collection officers make daily collections. Such microfinance plans now exist in India too. On the government's side, schemes like MUDRA loans have been launched.

What's fascinating about all this is that the huge barrier between capital and labor is breaking down. New possibilities are opening up. The Lijjat Papad cooperative was started by seven women. Now, 45,000 women work there, and they are all owners. Surely you've heard of the Gujarat Cooperative Milk Marketing Federation's Amul brand. Last year, their annual revenue was 800 billion rupees. Today, 36.4 lakh dairy farmers are associated with it. Three visionary men - Tribhuvandas Patel, Dr. H.M. Dalaya, and Dr. Verghese Kurien - built Amul.

Does your MBA college inspire you to do something so great? Similarly, look at Karnataka Milk Federation with its brand Nandini. After Amul, it is the country's second-largest milk cooperative, with 25.9 lakh members. Today, India is the world's largest milk producer. Those who say socialism only leads to poverty, these cooperatives are a fitting response to them.

Some great leaders have contributed to this, those who stepped out of the rat race for money and power and had an extraordinary vision. Today, what do we hear from every party politician in every election campaign? The names of the schemes may be different, but in essence, it's about directly putting money in people's pockets. This can be an effective measure in specific circumstances, but surely more can be done, where the central or state governments actually facilitate employment and empower people to contribute to the country's economy.

A businessman exploits apple farmers by buying their apples at very cheap rates. Farmers don't have cold storage; if they don't sell their apples, they'll rot. So they must take whatever price is offered. They take a loaded wheat trolley to the mandi; there's no option to take it back home. They must accept whatever price they get. If we look at how the government job salaries and the prices of goods have increased over the past 50 years, the MSP of crops has increased little in comparison. Even whatever meagre MSP exists, even that is not always received. Garlic and onions have had to be sold at 50 paise per kilo. If this isn't blackmail, what is? Capitalism claims to offer a free market, but what freedom does the farmer have in this system?

Can the government not form a cooperative of 500 apple growers? Can the government not build cold storage for farmers? If freezers can reach every shop in the country to store cola drinks, ice cream, and chocolate for companies, why can't innovative ideas be used to store farmers' vegetables? Can thousands of local vegetable markets not be established where farmers can sell directly to consumers?

Today, private companies have developed apps to connect taxi drivers with passengers. There are food delivery apps to link restaurants with customers. So why can't there be an app to connect farmers directly with consumers?

A farmer needs only 5-6 families to consume the wheat from his one field. If he has a flour mill at home, he can deliver fresh flour to these families every 15 days. When this idea came to my mind, I worked with a YouTuber to realize it for a farmer. We gave him a flour mill and helped him find the first five customers. Earlier, he sold wheat at 20 rupees per kg, from which, after deducting costs, he barely saved 10 rupees. Now he sells flour at 45 rupees per kg. We tripled his income. Why can't the government implement this model for millions of farmers?

Village folks can make many food items like gajjak, gajarpak, laddu, puffed rice balls, and pickles. With a week or two of training, they could even make bread, biscuits, and chips - without any maida or preservatives, so they're healthy. Besides food items, they can make cots, tables, chairs, bamboo stool, flutes, bags, baskets, earthen pitchers, utensils, idols, dolls, clothes, kurta, pants, suits, saree, necklaces, sweaters, jerseys, blankets, mats, and the list goes on. Within a month's training, they could learn to make soaps and shampoos. There are also skilled musicians and puppeteers. But they do not know much about marketing; they do not know how to advertise on Instagram or list their products on Amazon, Flipkart, or Myntra.

If the government wanted, it could assess which goods the country has to import. Many of those goods could be manufactured domestically. Also, which items could be exported abroad? Production planning can be done accordingly. Everyone in the country could be engaged in some form of employment. This would eradicate poverty. Health and education standards would improve. Pollution would be less with such a khadi industry. People could work while staying in their villages and homes, so cities wouldn't be overcrowded. People would feel a sense of community. Every problem could be solved this way. Politicians have made such promises but have never taken the trouble to implement the same.

Supposedly, in Gandhi's country, every politician respects the spinning wheel; there's the Ministry of Rural Development, the Khadi Department, Delhi Haat, various craft fairs, Khadi Bhavans; discussions about self-reliant India and being vocal for local; some of these things have been going on since Gandhi's time, but perhaps you have never used such a product yourself.

The Commerce Ministry released data that between April and September 2024, China remained our country's largest import source. Looking at the entire year, in 2023-24, India had a trade deficit with nine out of its top ten trading partners, meaning that we import more from them than we export. With China, this trade deficit was 85 billion dollars.

I'm not saying that you should hate every Chinese or any other country's person. A farmer in Shanghai has no personal quarrel with a farmer in Rohtak. Nor am I a staunch anti-globalist. But the question is, what about the common people of our country? Nationalism means all of us are one unit in this nation; So where does that nationalism go? The demand is in our country; products are sold here; our money is spent; but there's no employment for our own people.

Whenever development is discussed, they bring out the GDP rattle. The basic fact is ignored that India has the world's largest population; So, of course, overall GDP will be high. But if you look at GDP per capita, our country ranks 129th.

Unemployment in the country is no secret. GDP is rising, but whose pockets is the money going into? Wealth inequality is at its highest in a hundred years. When leaders from other countries come, walls are built to hide poverty.

When it comes to ease of doing business, convenience is always for billionaire tycoons. Highways are built for the trucks carrying their goods, but the roads in villages and towns are broken. Systems for taxes, registration, and so on are so complicated that an ordinary person becomes anxious before they even start a business. Municipal officials, police inspectors, sanitary inspectors - officials like these come to extort from the poor.

Where politicians should focus on bridging this gap of inequality by promoting small businesses, what we see instead is crony capitalism, where billionaires give campaign finances to the politicians and in return, they are awarded government contracts and loans from public sector banks. When you have no vision for the majority of the people in the country, then what kind of development is this? What kind of patriotism is this?

Our country has the world's largest market; there are millions of hardworking people here; many of the world's most brilliant minds come from here; we have mountains, deserts, seas, rivers, and forests. There is a wide variety of minerals. There are different seasons, many types of climates. So many kinds of fruits, grains, and vegetables are grown here. There are so many languages and diverse cultures. There is scope for tourism. If any country can truly be self-reliant, it is India. There is nothing lacking in our country.

It would not be an exaggeration to say that any government can turn the country into paradise within two years. The problem is, how do we bring about such a government?

People are divided along religious and caste lines; they vote along those lines. They are not educated, not sensible, and that's why there are uneducated people in Parliament too; many have criminal cases against them; legislators are ready to be bought.

In West Bengal, the Communist Party of India remained in power for so long. But they had no vision. Everything was ruined. Mamata Banerjee rose against them, but what did she really achieve? In Himachal Pradesh, there is a Congress government. Congress ruled Rajasthan for so many years. In Uttar Pradesh and Madhya Pradesh, the BJP is in power. In Punjab, the Aam Aadmi Party is governing, which also held power in Delhi for ten years. In Bihar, there has been a constant shift of power between RJD and JDU. In Tamil Nadu, sometimes it's the AIADMK, sometimes the DMK.

I am not saying that no party has done any work at all. Whether at the centre or in the states, every party has done something; reforms have been introduced. But is there any case study of any politician who has dramatically reduced poverty and unemployment; who has provided excellent government schools, libraries, hospitals, roads, electricity, water, clean air, and employment in any area; who has transformed the fate of farmers; who has totally eradicated crime?

Now it has come down to this: instead of those devilish politicians who incite people to fight among themselves, we have to choose the least bad option. For now, that is all the remaining hope I have from politicians. The public too doesn't have much expectation from anyone; now they don't even demand much. Even in the speeches and promises of politicians, there is no vision to be heard. You must have seen the election campaigns of the BJP, Congress, and Aam Aadmi Party in the recent Delhi elections. There really wasn't much difference in their campaign promises; nothing to suggest that any one party had any extraordinary vision.

Forget about the politicians, why spoil your mood? You tell me, what is your vision? If you are wealthy, or you are middle class and have some surplus left from your salary, you can start a small enterprise yourself. You can go on Shark Tank. You can employ many people. You can fix the 'trickle down' that hasn't happened in the economy; you can join the mission to decentralize the economy. You can be part of Gandhi's dream of 'Gram Swaraj' (village self-governance).

A child leaves the village for the city to study, to earn, to get ahead in life. Will he, once grown, say – 'Let's go back to the village'? When you see Mohan Bhargav in the film 'Swades', do you find it all just filmy melodrama, or those scenes actually touch you deep inside? Does the path of patriotism somewhere intersect with the path of your dreams? What are your dreams?

□□

Chapter - 8

Resonance of Scented Dreams

These days, motivation is being offered everywhere to achieve dreams, but what exactly are those dreams? Are they just dreams of winning the rat race? Is there anything dreamy in those dreams? Is there any ethereal element in them? Any innate beauty, imagination, resonance? Resonance is very important. Something that makes you feel fragrant from within. The rat race has it all - greed, competition, envy, toxic work culture, boredom, consumption, attention - everything except that fragrance.

There's no fragrance in personal dreams, and that fragrance is missing even in the model of patriotism we see nowadays. It's nice that on 15th August and 26th January we play patriotic songs, but if that fragrance was real, then why would we talk about patriotism only for two days? Being patriotic should be cool all year round. Whatever we might write on Instagram or Facebook, when it comes to close interactions with friends, we don't see any discussion about how to make the country better. If you try to start such a conversation, people make fun of you. We don't see patriotism as a surge coming from deep within the heart; we see it as a responsibility, a moral burden.

In fact, patriotism is not a natural emotion; love is a natural emotion. When you live with your family, you love your family. When you live with your village, you love your village.

My village was almost like a communist village. Everyone had their own houses, but the playground was shared. The wells and ponds were shared. There were three temples, and they belonged to everyone. When there was a religious feast at the temples, it was funded by everyone together. People served food to each other, and irrespective of whether someone was rich or poor, everyone sat on the ground to eat.

When the swang troupe came to perform folk theatre, everyone used to watch, even if someone had no money. Those who had more money would give rewards according to their capacity. Still, this didn't entitle anyone to a front-row seat. When the bicycle stunt master came, it was the same. Someone would give him a shirt and a pair of pants; someone would give him money; someone would even gift a clay pot for his performance.

When we went to the fields, if a tube well was running in any field, we would bathe in the large basin beneath it. We never felt the need to ask for permission. If the owner showed up, he would ask, "Have you finished bathing? Should I turn it off now?" If someone wanted to contest the MLA elections from the village, people contributed according to their capacity.

If there was a wedding in someone's house, it would be held in the community hall. Whether it was a feast at the temple or a wedding function, people ate according to their hunger, but when it came to giving money for a girl's wedding or donating for the feast, it was done as per one's capacity. If someone had more, they gave more. If not, no problem. For the wedding, LPG cylinders would be gathered from the neighborhood. Chairs, beds, and mattresses for guests came from the neighbors as well. Seven days before the wedding, women would start singing songs. They would visit the bride's home, sing, and dance. Boiled chickpeas and sweets would be distributed among them. The groom's wedding procession would pass through half the village, finally reaching the temple. Everyone would dance there.

If someone died, the bier was prepared by others. Even the funeral pyre was assembled by others. For thirteen days, people would visit their house to share their sorrow and comfort them.

Someone would sew clothes for someone else. Be it the daily necessities or livelihood, celebrations, mourning, or festivals, nothing was possible without the village. It's true that there was casteism in the village; life was not easy for women; improvements were needed there. But everything else was good. Every aspect of life was connected to the community. That's why there was love in the community, and people genuinely cared for each other.

Different relatives lived in other villages, so we'd visit other districts of our state as well. Same language, same culture across the state. So love grew from one's village to the entire state. And then, if you study about the country properly instead of rote learning in school, travel to different parts of the country, meet its people, read newspapers to understand their issues, learn about states from Punjab to Manipur, then that love can expand to the entire nation. And when you read world literature, read both Premchand and Franz Kafka; if you have learned from the Buddha and also from Socrates; if you watch brilliant films from world cinema, understand world history in detail, read about their issues in newspapers, you begin to relate to the whole world. Relations are built through relating. Only then does the ideal of "Vasudhaiva Kutumbakam"– the world is one family– come true. This is the highest state of humanity. Bhagat Singh wrote beautifully about this in his article "Vishva Prem" (Universal Love).

This is what Advaita philosophy is: where you make no distinction between yourself and others. If you're a believer, you see yourself and everyone else as manifestations of the same Brahman. If you're an atheist, you see them as people just like yourself; you must have that empathy within you.

When such fragrant humanity fills you from within, then patriotism too has a fragrance. Doing something for the nation becomes a beautiful adventure. It brings joy. It guides every decision you make.

I received an offer to direct a film. The story was about a woman having an affair with her husband's friend and then getting her husband murdered. It was a crime thriller. The writer of the story was also the producer. I said, "Already, so many negative things are said about women; is it right to make another film like this?" He replied, "No, it's not like that; all kinds of women exist; this is based on a true story from my village." I thought, okay, let's do it. After all, I'd be writing the screenplay; so I could ensure it wasn't a film prejudiced against women, but rather something sensitive and meaningful about human nature.

But he refused to give me full control over the screenplay. He kept narrating scenes with conviction; there was some odd joke at one place, because he felt comic relief was necessary; somewhere he placed a folk song: "Woh nirbhaag lugai hoti hai" (That kind of woman is the jinxed one).

I asked for time to consider. Two days later, I sent an audio message politely declining, saying, "You've thought deeply about this; if I make changes, it won't feel right; maybe we can work together on something else some other day."

To be honest, I was very keen to make a film at that time, but it just didn't feel right. It wasn't as if I felt some huge patriotic burden while refusing. I simply wouldn't enjoy making a film with that kind of screenplay.

Dhruv was offered one crore rupees for a brand advertisement. It wasn't for a cola or chips ad, which is harmful to health. It was for hair oil. Dhruv declined simply because their advertisement made pseudo-scientific claims. It's not like Dhruv has 500 crores with him. One crore was a huge amount for him too. But he didn't feel as if he had made a great sacrifice for the nation by refusing. He just didn't feel like doing it.

He's had offers from online betting apps, and even Bigg Boss. Dhruv didn't have the slightest hesitation in refusing any such offers.

When you walk the right path, humanity, quest for meaningfulness, and patriotism become a part of your mind and character. Then you naturally care about the youth of your country, that if they get into online betting, they will lose their way. You simply don't feel like endorsing such ads.

Osho says that 'selfishness' is a beautiful word; it just fell into the wrong hands. 'Swarth' means 'swa' (self) + 'arth' (meaning), that is, your own meaning, your own purpose. Why would anyone do anything that has no meaning for them? If there's no 'arth' (meaning), there will be 'anarth' (ruin). The problem is that people do not know their true self-interest. They're chasing things that will ultimately bring only sorrow, no satisfaction.

If you run in the rat race, with the idea that you must acquire wealth by any means, then your dreams and your patriotism end up in opposition to each other. Then you feel that your own self-interest and dream is just to have lots of money, but should you sacrifice it for patriotism?

Even then, there's a calculation: will this sacrifice give me good PR, and will that PR help me earn even more money later?

Superstars get amazing PR from their NGOs. Their crimes are overlooked because someone from a slum appears on TV saying that "bhai" helped them with money. 'Brother' may make terrible films, may be accused of murder, but he has a golden heart! Even a useless influencer gets amazing PR: look how he is distributing blankets among the poor!

A rich businessman hands out money to Instagram influencers for his PR. Then the influencers show how generous the businessman is, feeding the poor with his own hands. Scams and frauds worth thousands of millions get hidden behind this PR.

In this way, corporate philanthropy is not against capitalism and the market economy; it is a part of it. It is just a makeshift form of repentance, excellent PR. If I were in government, the first thing I'd do is end this charade of corporate social responsibility. There would be no such government rule or law. If a corporation truly wants to do good, let them do so, but nobody gets any tax breaks.

This is not just the model of the rich and superstars; it applies on a smaller scale to you as well. Even for you, there's no fragrance in social service; it's not part of your dreams. And if it is, then tell me: do you and your friends talk more about property rates, the stock market, phones and car models, or do you ever actually discuss social service? Venting frustration about the country's problems is a different thing– we all do that. But have you ever genuinely discussed what to do for society?

Whenever you've thought, "let's do something super fun today," has that ever included going on a hunger strike to get a road built, or making twenty kids in a slum fluent in English?

When you do social service, when you become an activist, you are doing something for the people of the country. So it is not separate from patriotism. But it is the very opposite of the rat race.

You run the rat race, but occasionally, compassion knocks at your heart. You feel a bit of inner conflict, so you give ten rupees to a beggar at a red light signal. You think, "This is all I can do. Anyway, no one does good these days. Why should I be the only one to make an effort? What can I achieve all by myself?"

Then, when you see someone doing something for society, it's as if their goodness becomes a mirror for you. You start finding flaws in them. Superstars have plenty of money and fame; they're also in the race of the prison just like you; one day, you'll also start an NGO and distribute blankets like the superstar– so you have no problem with him. But when a boy earning 40,000 rupees a month is undertaking a cleanliness drive somewhere on the weekend or planting trees, you think, "If I can't do it, then how is he able to do something?" That boy has shaken your system. You find fault in him, saying, "He talks about saving the environment, then why doesn't he live in a hut himself?"

Shiv Vats, a government school teacher, appears on Instagram (@englishwalesirrr). In his reels, he is seen teaching children in creative ways. You think he's just making content; his real motive isn't to teach kids but to become famous. The foolish influencer posting reels about distributing blankets doesn't bother you because he's rich, famous, and in your race. But you don't like this energetic government school teacher.

If someone quits a job to become a saint, debates start. If someone leaves a job to start organic farming, you say it's just a trend now; it's all nonsense. But if that person starts earning 10 crore rupees from it, you'd be ready to consider him an inspiration.

In the end, it always comes back to money. The desire for money isn't wrong, but if that desire becomes the primary goal, then it's a problem.

I wish that I earn 500 crores and Dhruv earns another 500 crores so that all the money isn't in the hands of those running in the prison race. More money should be in the hands of those who use it properly, who have fascinating dreams. I would love to create avenues for independent films, for local films. I dream of a publishing house that can publish novels written by the poor deriving inspiration from their lived experience. They would put in their struggles and joys with authenticity, in their colloquial language, and these novels could then act as a catharsis for other poor people. Dhruv dreams of doing so much more to save the environment besides making YouTube videos.

You dreamed of a bungalow for yourself, with a gym, a swimming pool, and a home theater. But have you ever dreamed of a village that's very clean and beautiful? Every house has flowers outside its windows; there are trees on the streets, bearing apples that anyone could pluck and eat. There's a cycling track on the side of the road. No pollution. During the day, the sky appears deep blue. At night, the sky is filled with stars. There's no traffic noise because people don't honk. Surrounding the village are fields, and there are parks in the residential areas, where people can exercise and kids can play. There's a top-level school, a hospital, markets, cafes, and restaurants.

If villages like that existed, even cities wouldn't be crowded. Instead of a 'global village,' if the globe were a collection of such beautiful villages and towns, then the whole world would be beautiful– a big group of tiny heavens. This model isn't wholly communism, socialism, or capitalism. But what difference does that make! Whatever you call it, the point is that it's beautiful!

I don't know about you, but if there's an option– either I own a palace surrounded by poverty, unemployment, and pollution, or I have a simple home in such a village– I would have no confusion at all in choosing. But is such a village even possible?

I dreamed of this, and then I actually saw this dream come true. A village in Russia. That village was exactly like the heaven I just described.

We cycled for two hours in the morning and reached the nearby village. People there didn't speak English. But they had such patience that I would speak in English to the Google Translate app on my phone, which would translate into Russian; then they'd read the Russian text and reply in Russian, and after reading the English translation, I would again ask them for some clarification. When we got off the bus, we asked someone for directions. That person put his daughter on his shoulder and walked alongside us. He guided us to the lodge and then went his way.

I have seen such peace and humility also in Himachal and Sikkim villages. When life is peaceful, peace enters people's minds too– peace filled with a lovely fragrance.

Fake gurus talk about peace, but that peace isn't fragrant. It's like a temporary medicine. When a person running the prison race gets overwhelmed by stress, experiences anxiety, gets bored with consumption, he goes to an ashram in the mountains seeking spiritual healing, a retreat, or a week-long meditation course to get the vibration of the universe. I exposed all that vibration mumbo-jumbo in the previous e-book, 'Power of the Universe.'

Anyway, leaving aside fake gurus, there is a problem with the genuine spiritual teachers as well: they don't speak of joy. People have taken their lifetime memberships. So many engineers graduate from the engineering colleges every year; doctors graduate from the medical colleges; lawyers from the law schools. But the guru's spiritual college has only one graduate– himself. No one else has received an enlightenment degree to date.

Guruji says many good things; he doesn't spread superstitions or pseudoscience. But he's not working in a toxic work culture; he's sitting amidst nature giving sermons. But those who follow him have to go back to their jobs afterward.

That person goes to the mall to entertain himself, and Guruji disapproves of this. He says-

Why are you stuck in this useless glitter? Shopping, this stuff, this pretence– that's the illusory world of maya. That's why global warming is increasing; carbon footprints are rising; the Earth is being destroyed.

That's true. So, should we stop shopping and just drink beer?

Not at all. That's not only harmful to health but also corrupts religion. A person loses his consciousness.

Should we eat chicken or fish tikka?

That's violence inflicted on the animal, which now enters your own body.

So let's relish some shahi paneer?

No, using dairy products is also violence against animals. Be vegan.

Let me have delicious Veg makhanwala or mushroom tikka.

O devilish man, control your senses. Eat so that you can live; don't make your life all about eating.

Should I get a new hairstyle?

Why are you stuck on outer beauty!

Oh, then I'll watch stand-up comedy?

Do you plan to waste your time on this banter? There's a conspiracy to keep you entangled in this.

Should I surf social media?

There's just garbage there.

Let me watch a good movie?

Those movies will only brainwash you. Anyway, why does your mind need so much entertainment?

Go to a disco, a club, dance there?

There's noise in your mind. That's why you need the noise of a club.

Festivals are coming; I'll eat sweets.

You're disrespecting the sanctity of festivals, turning them into just an occasion to eat sweets.

My girlfriend is calling me.

That love is fake; it's all deception. It's just lust, and lust is like a prison. Look at other animals; do they ever mate so much?

Feeling lonely, I'll meet friends.

No, why meet friends to get rid of loneliness? Eradicate the loneliness within you.

So what to do, Guru ji? You should only guide me.

Move towards self-realization.

Okay, and then?

First, do this.

I'm not enjoying this, Guru ji. After five days of such torture at the office, I absolutely don't want this. I want some fun.

Get lost from here, fool. You'll find pleasure in drugs. So why not take drugs?

Your point is also true, Guru ji. Drugs ruin life. But I need some fun in life. You tell me which fun is right.

You will experience the supreme bliss of truth. The darkness of ignorance will be eradicated. You will merge into the Supreme.

This can't be achieved by ordinary people. Listening to Guru ji's words, they feel that their stress level is reduced; they feel more calm than before, but there is no fun here.

I had some fun. Wait, not fun; what I felt was ultimate bliss. How to describe what it was? It was such a high. Ah, the word 'high' has been degraded. Think of it as losing oneself. Like you might have seen Sufi saints dancing in circles in devotion; or imagine Archimedes shouting "Eureka!" when the displacement theory struck him in the bathtub. Or perhaps you've seen a peacock dancing joyfully in the jungle. Oh, but when did anyone see a peacock dance in the jungle? Good that no one saw, otherwise people would start clicking photos, and that would disturb the dance. How would the peacock dance so carefree then?

I didn't perform a play in the jungle; I did it in the college auditorium; in six colleges including ours. In the play, someone was about to be hanged. I played the role of a prison guard who had to help the executioner. It was the first time for the prison guard; he was nervous, but the executioner had been doing this for years. He didn't read newspapers; he didn't know the prisoners' names. Every prisoner was just a number to him. But this time, the prisoner turned out to be the long-lost son of the executioner, who had run away from home long ago. It was revealed because the prisoner sent a beautiful watch for the executioner, and the executioner had the same watch.

When I wandered anxiously in the prison, shouting, asking why I had to do this, what my fault was, the entire auditorium echoed with applause. In theatre, an actor can have two goals: one is to give such a powerful performance that people are deeply affected and applaud; that's where the thrill of getting attention lies. People are applauding for you, praising you - ego is satisfied. The second goal is that the actor shouldn't be affected by the applause; he should fully lose himself, so much so that the audience forgets to applaud.

I asked the executioner what the time was. He checked his watch and told the time. I remarked, "Amazing! To check the time of someone's hanging, there is such a beautiful watch!" The audience laughed together. When the executioner told his personal story, complete silence prevailed. Hundreds of people present, but pin-drop silence.

At that moment, we actors weren't separate; we had become one. The ones sitting at the lights and the ones handling the music, they too had become one with us. We had become one play. The executioner shared his sorrow, remembered his son, his eyes had dried like stone, and tears flowed from the audience's eyes. The audience also had become one with the play.

There was a resonance here; a perfect frequency match. No, not some supernatural vibration or energy like the fake godmen talk about. Then what was it? It's hard to explain; you have to feel it for yourself sometime.

I felt such resonance sitting among the audience when I heard Kishori Amonkar sing at Delhi's Nehru Park. Initially, I wasn't particularly interested in classical music. I only attended events like these in my college organized by 'SPIC MACAY' just for compering, because I loved to compere. Slowly, that's how my interest grew.

Then I started going to concerts and listened to the country's best singers live: Pandit Jasraj, Ustad Rashid Khan, Shubha Mudgal, Jagjit Singh, the Wadali Brothers… And one day, I heard Kishori Amonkar. It was in the evening. People were sitting on white sheets in the park. The notes began to flow. There wasn't any deep philosophy. It was simply Radha's melancholic call. She tells her friend that since Shyam left, she's been restless. Can you feel that ache? Have you ever felt such deep love? When you see the 'love' of 'Kabir Singh' in a cinema hall, how would you grasp the two-and-a-half characters of Kabir's love? How could you truly feel Radha's profound love when you see Radhe of 'Tere Naam'?

Kishori Amonkar was attempting to do such magic– to make this feeling dissipate into the air like gulaal. There were just three or four lines in the bandish, which she sang for forty minutes. Just as a lover in longing doesn't write essays, but instead repeats the same phrases in their yearning. That is the very concept of 'khayal' singing - to give voice to that emotion so that the listener could feel that longing within themselves. At first, I just admired Kishori Amonkar in my heart, thinking that this is why she's called the Saraswati of singing. The audience would intermittently applaud. Then the applause stopped.

Osho says, "Dance in such a way that the dancer disappears, only the dance remains." There, too, the singer and the singing had become one. The audience was falling into a kind of trance. I had become music. The trees, the grass, everything had become music. Resonance.

In an interview, Arijit Singh once said that classical music can never be mainstream. It's not just idle entertainment; it's deeply internal; it's a form of meditation. He is right. Not everything is for everyone. Only those willing to dive into the depths of the ocean find the rarest pearls. If you have never felt goosebumps while listening to music, then what kind of music have you heard?

It is not necessary that you listen to Indian classical music only; you can listen to Western classical– Beethoven, Chopin, or Mozart; Kurt Cobain or Led Zeppelin; Begum Akhtar or Mehdi Hassan; Abida Parveen or Nusrat Fateh Ali Khan; Mohammad Rafi or Kishore Kumar. But there should be something of depth. If a person drowns, then it is in the sea only; how can someone drown in a shallow pool?

The mathematics syllabus can be very boring. But if you get engrossed in a puzzle to the extent that every fiber of your being is devoted to solving it, you experience depth. Watch the film 'The Man Who Knew Infinity' based on the great mathematician Ramanujan's life. There's a beautiful scene where Ramanujan is walking at night along the seashore with his wife. She asks him about his research. Ramanujan picks up some soil and asks her what it is; she replies it's soil. He then says -

"Imagine if we could look so closely, we could see each grain, each particle. You see, there are patterns in everything- the colors of the night, the reflections on water. In mathematics, these patterns reveal themselves in the most incredible form, and it's kind of beautiful."

People say that Newton understood gravity when an apple fell on his head; So for all those years, when he went to the bathroom, was his urine flying toward the ceiling? Whoever said that, meant it as a joke, but the question is valid. Will someone become a scientist just because an apple hit their head? Many people have probably had apples or other things fall on them, but they didn't discover the law of gravity. The thing is, Newton was lost in thought - there was a flood of ideas rushing through his mind. The falling of the apple was the final moment– like someone striking at a wall for a week and finally landing the blow that brings it down.

Similarly, Archimedes must have stepped into the bathtub many times before. But when your mind is preoccupied with something, simply sitting in the tub could become a "Eureka" moment. An apple falling on the head becomes a Eureka moment.

When you sit down to write poetry, sometimes nothing comes to your mind. And at other times, an entire poem appears in a single flash. As Ghalib said, "These ideas come to the mind from the unseen." What is this unseen, this miracle? Sometimes it's an emotional surge that bursts forth as poetry. There was a time in college when my mind was very unsettled. A senior said, "Your name is Vijeta; it seems you're not taking your name seriously these days." His words struck me; I felt like, sure, I'm enjoying life, but what about my life's purpose? What about my dreams? Sitting on the college ground, this came to mind -

To spend away life isn't the purpose
Life will pass anyhow even if in vain

Worries of daily life and mourning over love
Ah! there must be something else to gain

That old sense of adventure surrounds me
A new tune plays in my heart yet again

Why are you running, people ask me
A surge of dreams runs in my vein

It's not necessary for a poet to personally experience happiness, sorrow, or turmoil. The poet relates to society, observes deeply, reads the minds of others. He can feel the pain of others and their joy. William Wordsworth visited a village with his sister, saw a woman harvesting in a field, and wrote 'The Solitary Reaper.' Nirala wrote 'Woh Todti Pathar' (She breaks Stones). Nagarjun saw in the robust, mustachioed face of a bus driver a father whose daughter had hung her pink bangles on the bus before her father's eyes, whose eyes shone with milky parental affection; and he described this feeling in his poem 'Gulabi Choodiyan' (Pink Bangles). Its very simplicity gives it an innocence - what the driver felt, what Nagarjun felt, you feel the same emotion in your own heart. That same twinkle appears in your eye. Resonance.

That's what artists - writers, poets, actors, musicians, painters - experience. We all have the familiar image of the 'crazy scientist' lost in his own world. But besides artists and scientists, what about everyone else?

Can there be resonance while making momos? Can you find meditation in mayonnaise? Think about it. It sounds funny. Meditation - something so deep and spiritual. While momos are made of refined flour, deep-fried in oil, full of MSG, slathered in mayonnaise - a seeming hallmark of indulgence. Something that just pleases the palate and the senses. What connection could there be between the two?

But if you don't add mayonnaise and MSG, use whole wheat flour instead of refined flour, steam them instead of deep frying, and make them at home for your family, could there be meditation in making momos then? The process is still the same. If there can be meditation in making wheat momos, then why not in making refined flour ones? Just think about it.

Celebrity chef Ranveer Brar gave an interview to Neelesh Misra. He was asked what food means to him. This was his reply -

"For me, food is an ever-evolving relationship. It's the most important relationship of my life. Today, food is both an expression and a responsibility for me. Food is now my primary partner, and I am the minor partner. I am merely its mouthpiece... My grandmother's shawl smelt of milk and ghee. And sometimes cardamom, which she'd tie in a corner of her scarf. Sometimes whole spices... If you've spent so many years at it, you can't leave these things undefined, but you can't entirely define them either. So what words do you give to food? I leave it open for others to interpret. Today, this is what food means to me. Maybe tomorrow it will be something else."

Don't focus right now on what he meant. Just think - have you seen anyone look at food this way? Or talk about food in this way? Or feel about food like this?

He then talks about cooking: every finger has a 'rasa' (essence); the home of rasa is called 'rasvati,' which is where the word 'rasoi' (kitchen) comes from. And rasa is a matter of perception, just like music. And you have to think about the person who eats the food; you have to get inside their mind. So you create the space for rasa in your own mind. And this selfless consideration for the person who will eat it is the foundation. Your relationship with the one you feed is the basis. There is an inherent joy in creating something for them.

Ranveer then explains how cooking is a unique art form -

"I sculpt, I paint a little, I even write some poetry. But for me, the ultimate expression is when someone consumes something with all their senses. And I'm proud that I'm associated with an art form that no one else can touch. Because now, I am becoming a part of you. As they say, what are we after all, but food."

Don't worry for now about whether poetry is a better art form, or cinema, or cooking. Is it even right to call cooking an art form? These questions aren't necessary. What matters is the kind of deep, passionate sentiment Ranveer holds towards cooking.

It's not just something he says on a podcast; he gives a real-life example. Many chefs come to him to work with him in a restaurant or on a TV show. They come prepared, wanting to whip up some fancy Michelin-worthy dish. But Ranveer simply asks them to make dal tadka and aloo jeera. And through this, he can tell how much they really know, because when there are fewer ingredients, your presence and your relationship with the food comes through. He has another test: making tea. Give two people the same pots, the same stove, the same amount of milk, the same tea leaves, everything exactly the same. The tea will still turn out different. Because in the process, you react when the aroma arises, how dark the color gets, when the milk should be added. That's why tea is a reflection of how well you react in the moment and how active your senses are while making it.

Ranveer is a celebrity chef. He has hosted many cooking shows on TV and has been a judge on the 'Master Chef India' show. He has written two books and acted in two films. Today, he has restaurants all over the world, which means he is also a businessman. Yet, he still talks about cooking. Even now, he often cooks by himself. He grow's vegetables at his home. He talks about the evolution of food as to how food has never remained the same, it keeps evolving, but this evolution should be organic. To illustrate this, he goes back to 1850, when Warren Hastings allotted land to a Chinese man, Tong Achee, to set up a sugar factory. That's why sugar is called 'cheeni' in

India. He talks about the slow food movement, meaning whether it is about growing food or cooking it, we should give it time.

Now, contrast this with a man who wants to quit his job and start a momo stall for a living. He found two cooks from somewhere. He just started making whatever is trending. In most food stalls, roadside dhaba, or restaurants, you see these days: make items with refined flour, add loads of ketchup, dump in some cheese, add ajinomoto, loads of butter, salt, and sugar, dump in a ton of spices. Whether it's kesar rasmalai, jalebi, or green chutney, they put artificial colors in everything. They put orange-colored cola in the spicy water of gol-gappa. They add heaps of refined flour to soya chaap. There is even news now of vendors adding acid to make gol-gappa water more spicy, or urea and palm oil being added to synthetic paneer. That clearly falls into the illegal category, but even with the rest of the food, does it have a purpose, passion, or relationship with food that is seen in Ranveer Brar's approach? Not at all.

So, the point is not whether the momos are made of refined flour or wheat flour, the point is the mindset. Do you want to enjoy the art of creating amazing food? Are you interested in letting people experience wonderful flavors? Not just the taste, but the whole experience, which includes the way the food is served and even the decor of the restaurant. Or is it just a way to run the rat race for money? Change your perspective, and the whole view changes. For some, cooking is a headache; for others, it's a meditation.

We can see the same thing happening in the field of education. Byju's has been accused of financial fraud and using unethical sales practices. For instance, poor parents have been intimidated into buying courses by being told that if they don't, their children's futures will be ruined. In Kota, students prepare for engineering and medical entrance exams. A report from May 4 tells us that 14 students have died by suicide in just the first four months of 2025. This has been going on for years. Civil Services offer fewer than a thousand vacancies, but 6-7 lakh students across the country take the exam. Mukherjee Nagar is a hub for this coaching, and like Kota, depression is common here as well. Students lose several years in the preparation; they live here in small, dingy rooms -- like pigeonholes. In one coaching center, the basement flooded and three students drowned.

Think about how beautiful education is! We worship it in the form of Saraswati. But do you see any beauty in these places? Here, students no longer show a curiosity to learn new things; instead, there is a thirst for jobs, money, and status. Teachers aren't excited to spread the light of knowledge, but are entirely focused on producing top rankers and increasing sales. Having a teaching job in these institutes is just another part of that prison.

Teaching, though, can also be a meditation. I have a friend who is a farmer and lives in a village in Haryana. I was surprised to hear his daughter speak fluent English. His son was solving math problems quickly. How did this happen? My friend told me that three brothers from Bihar had moved to their village and started living there on rent. They began teaching village kids, charging low fees. As a result, the children are doing better academically and learning to speak English. Not just that, these teachers also make the children exercise. They instill good values, teaching them that using abusive language is wrong and that they should stay away from any kind of intoxicants. Here, you see that image of a teacher who is revered. These three brothers are shaping the children's lives, uplifting the entire generation of the village. They're on a mission.

Many government school teachers are known for their idleness. They have no enthusiasm. But I have a friend whose students are now employed in various jobs. These students were poor and lived in slums; if the teacher hadn't been good, hadn't sparked their interest in studies, or hadn't shown them any dreams, those students might have dropped out, remained unemployed, or even turned to crime. But now they have jobs, have come out of their slum's poverty, and even after many years, they haven't forgotten their teacher. For my friend, teaching is his meditation.

For Abhishek Banerjee, acting is meditation. You must know him as the main villain in 'Paatal Lok'. He says that the best thing about being an actor is that he forgets all his personal problems and enters the world created by the writer and director. Nawazuddin Siddiqui said in an interview that he also does films for money so that he can do good films like 'Manto' for free. Daniel Day-Lewis went and lived in the jungle for six months to prepare for one role. On the other hand, there are superstars who don't even try to act. They've earned hundreds of crores; they could produce films with challenging roles for themselves but have no such desire. All they want is to earn 500 or 600 crores. Despite being actors, their joy is still limited to consumption and attention. Make money and go on luxury cruises; fans take their autographs; they appear in newspapers; they want attention; awards can be bought; that's all there is for them.

Similarly, for Kishori Amonkar, music could be a form of devotion. But then there are superstar singers who boast about how they fooled people, how their hit song made no sense; they just wrote something random in five minutes. Considering the prison race for money, they are smart and the audience is stupid because they made lots of money. But if you think about it, they never really experienced the magic of making music all these years. They claim that A.R. Rahman is their inspiration, but what inspiration did they take? Rahman composed timeless songs for countless films like 'Roja', 'Bombay', 'Dil Se', 'Swades', and 'Rockstar'; but have these singers ever made a single song that people would listen to even after ten years? So, it's possible that there is no resonance or deep feeling even for some artists, while for someone else, cooking can be a passion.

This applies to other professions as well. My brother is a lawyer. A boy once came to him; he had got admission to Oxford University on a government scholarship, but a bureaucrat created trouble by raising some petty objection. My brother fought his case, and the boy's name got back on the list. The government department challenged this decision in the High Court. The case was won again in the High Court. That boy finally went to Oxford University. In many such cases, my brother has helped people get justice. First, he feels good knowing someone's life has changed because of him. Second, he enjoys the process - getting to the root of a case, the legal maneuvers, arguing in court. Whereas there are lots of lawyers in court who are completely jaded; their life is the same; for them, there is nothing special about being a lawyer.

I'm giving examples from around me so you can look beyond the idol of Steve Jobs. Look around you too; you'll certainly find people who are honest in their work, take pride in it, and truly enjoy it; in this way, you can believe that joy is possible.

My wife teaches Hindi. The Hindi subject and Hindi teachers are generally considered very boring. But she thought, why not explain poetic devices using Bollywood songs as examples? For instance, she explained yamak (antanaclasis) with 'sajna hai mujhe sajna ke liye' (I have to groom myself to welcome my groom). The children enjoyed it, understood everything, and then even gave examples themselves. My wife's goal as a Hindi teacher is to spark enthusiasm for Hindi literature in her students.

While there are many Hindi teachers who only crammed the syllabus to pass the qualifying exam for the job, besides that, they have never read even one novel in their lives. Not a single poem outside the syllabus. They only chose Hindi as a subject because it gave them a better chance of getting a job. Like that superstar singer, these people even take pride in having taught nothing and still getting a salary. But what have they really gained from this? In the very work that could have given them life's purpose, peace, or passion, they just carry that work like a burden.

The same goes for farmers; they just go through the motions of farming. Hardly anyone wants to do farming these days. Those who get jobs lease out their lands. Those who farm do so under compulsion. Although films sing songs like 'Mere desh ki dharti sona ugle' (My country's soil yields gold), the truth is that farming is a lot of hard work with very little savings. Whatever the government should do but doesn't, we have already discussed that. But what are the farmers themselves doing?

To become an engineer, people study engineering. To be a doctor, lawyer, CA, manager, or musician, everyone studies for their field. But have you ever seen a farmer learning anything new? Just sow the seeds, put in DAP, urea, and that's it. Then spray pesticide once. After the harvest, burn the stubble. Heat up the land, kill the insects, destroy the soil's microbiome. Destroy the nitrogen, phosphorus, potassium, sulfur, and organic carbon in the soil. Next year, use even more chemical fertilizers. Go to the market to sell your produce, keep getting blackmailed. What have the farmers done to change their own conditions? Have they ever sought advice from an agricultural scientist at an agriculture fair? Ever tried to understand farming techniques? Ever thought about food processing?

Abhishek Dhama is a resident of Palla village near Delhi. His story was published in 'The Better India.' Abhishek's father was a farmer, but Abhishek didn't want to do that. Farmers themselves don't want their children to get into farming. Abhishek studied engineering in electronics and communication. He was interested in fitness, and always played cricket and volleyball. When he started building his body in the gym, he first learned about the importance of nutrition. He always knew that pesticides were used in fields, but after all this research, he realized how harmful they really are. But due to lack of expertise and experience, he didn't have the courage to start organic farming on his fields. So, he made a small vegetable garden. He watched many YouTube videos day and night. He grew traditional vegetables like tomatoes, bitter gourd, bottle gourd, radish, and some exotic vegetables like broccoli and red lettuce. He used some organic fertilizer in his garden and some crop residues. When the vegetables grew, their color and taste were much better than those found in the market. Abhishek felt some confidence. Now, he experimented on his family fields. He grew 'stevia,' a low-calorie alternative to sugar. The stevia also grew, but Abhishek failed to sell it. He suffered a loss. Neighboring farmers mocked him. When I met Abhishek once, he personally told me that wherever he went, people teased him by calling him 'stevia.'

But Abhishek tried one more time. This time, he focused on understanding not just farming but the market as well. He grew the same vegetables he had grown in his garden, but now using even better methods. For example, he started drip irrigation, which meant that water went directly to the roots of the plants. Ninety percent of the water was saved. It also took less time, which saved electricity. Since only the plant area was irrigated, weed growth became very minimal. By planting bamboo sticks at an eight-foot distance and tying wires, he made trellises for bottle gourd vines to climb. In this way, doing multi-layer farming, he got two crops from the same field. The vegetables grown above ground got less insect infestation; heavy downpour now caused less damage. Today, Abhishek earns in lakhs, because instead of dragging farming like a burden, he made it into a project, an adventure. He immersed himself completely in it.

He is an educated young man, but he is now listening to the story of Santosh Pachar, a woman from a village in Rajasthan who has only studied up to the eighth grade. She and her husband were troubled because the carrots in their field were crooked and not very tasty. Their income was so low that they could barely make ends meet. Santosh began attending agricultural fairs organized by the state government. She discovered that the problem was with their seeds. Based on whatever she understood, she conducted an experiment: she mixed the carrot seeds with three parts honey and one part desi ghee. From the carrots that grew, she used seeds from those carrots for the next harvest. After a few harvests, her carrots were much better in taste, shine, and size. As a result, their annual income increased twenty times. Later, she found out that what she had done was actually a scientific method to improve seed quality, known as grading. The state agricultural officials tested her seeds and declared them a new seed variety, which was named SPL 101. Santosh has been honored by the President in 2013 and 2017. Today, she has trained 7,000 farmers. We have become accustomed to seeing the image of a farmer as one of poverty, helplessness, and compulsion. But now look at this picture, full of enthusiasm, interest, and meditation.

Even in common jobs like farming, which are often done out of necessity, there can be some joy.

Sports are a career where passion for the game and excellence go hand in hand with money. You will play with total immersion and attention; only then will you play well, only then will you win; people will praise you, and there will be money. But to play well, you need many years of regular practice. What has happened now is that the IPL has turned cricketers into celebrities– advertisements, brand deals, interviews, money in crores. Kids think, "It's just playing after all." Sports are better than studies or office jobs; there's money and fame too. People think the same way about films.

But the truth is that whether it be sports or acting in films, both need years of training, hard work**,** and discipline. Also, not everyone can make a living out of such professions. Many people are drawn to their glitz and glamour, only to become disheartened. That's why badminton champion Pullela Gopichand said a few months ago that middle-class parents should not send their children into sports. For those who don't make it big, there is a severe lack of alternate careers. Even Olympic medalists who get jobs through the 'sports quota' struggle to find real respect there.

On the other hand, there are those who come into sports purely for the joy of playing. They think, "At least I enjoyed the game for a while; now, if there's no money here, let's do something else. I'll keep playing now as a hobby."

There are many such unconventional careers, some of which we mentioned earlier, which people pursue only if they're truly interested in them–

- Ornithologists who study birds,
- Paleontologists who study fossils and tell the Earth's history,
- Archaeologists who review history based on items found during excavations,
- Historians who study written material,
- Life coaches who listen, help you think logically, and untangle your life's problems,

- Designers who create company logos,
- Fashion designers who design clothes,
- Architects who design houses or buildings,
- Urban planners who plan the roads, parks, schools, and neighborhoods of new towns or cities,
- Film editors,
- Fashion photographers,
- Photojournalists,
- Journalists,
- Data scientists,
- Market researchers,
- Statisticians who turn health, education, employment, crime, company sales, and such things into numbers,
- Sociologists who study society and social behavior,
- Environmentalists working for the environment,
- And countless other such careers.

All these seem like jobs where a person can truly immerse themselves and enjoy the work. They can find a purpose in life. But these possibilities got drowned out in the clamour of "there's no scope." These careers were not considered good for the rat race. These possibilities were washed away by the hope of a million-rupee package in a manager's job and the prestige attached to becoming an IAS officer.

There's nothing wrong with a manager's job either, whether it's event management or production management in a company. Certainly, there are people who enjoy managing everything. They may find a job without a toxic work culture, where they can apply their innovative ideas and play a vital role in a company's growth. But the real question is: Did you choose this job based on your passion? Do you truly enjoy your work, or do you start waiting for Saturday as soon as Monday arrives? If you find joy in it, that's great.

The same applies to the IAS. We know many bureaucrats want to make big money and crave others' attention. Honest officers are very few. The ones who are honest, they get transferred every six months. Ashok Khemka is a popular example. He was transferred 57 times in a 34-year career. Still, there are many officers doing excellent work in their areas: some officer started a recycling revolution in Hyderabad; someone brought electricity and water to villages in Sikkim; someone got Indore the label of the cleanest city.

Speaking of the IPS, it is imperative to mention SP Jai Yadav. Even today, in many parts of the country, Dalits are not allowed to ride a horse at their wedding. In a district of Rajasthan, a Dalit said that he wanted to ride a horse at his wedding. He appealed to the district administration, asking them to ensure the rights granted to him by the Constitution of India. When the matter reached the police, Jai realized that merely providing police security would not be enough. Even if security was provided during the wedding, those people still had to live in the village after the wedding. Many people preparing for civil services do rot learning about Gandhi's movements, but Jai chose to use Gandhi's methods. He identified 25-30 villages where such inequality existed and then formed an Equality Committee in each village. This committee included the village head (sarpanch), two members from each caste, and police officers. These committees conducted awareness campaigns throughout the villages, spoke with people, and explained things to them. As a result, Dalit youths in these villages sat on horseback at their weddings, songs were played on DJ setups, and people from all castes attended the wedding. Imagine how a police officer altered the course of history, thus improving the present and the future of the people in these villages.

In civil services interviews, everyone gives idealistic answers. They say they have patriotic feelings and want to use their power to change the country. But some honest officers truly feel this in their hearts. They feel a sense of satisfaction seeing the impact of their work.

Anyway, not every job can bring joy. No matter how diligent you are, some jobs are just boring. Imagine how much a security guard standing at the mall entrance can truly immerse themselves in opening the door. Malls came with capitalism; restaurants followed, bringing with them gatekeepers who open doors for you; big offices brought reception desks, and along came receptionists. No matter how honestly you fill petrol at a pump in the scorching afternoon, what excellence or meditation can you bring to it? This is all a scam played on you.

Even in white-collar jobs, as we discussed earlier, some jobs separate you from your human essence. There's no creativity in the work; you do it just because the salary comes in, but the work has no real meaning in the world. You are separated from the product's design and process. You are alienated from your social nature through monotonous overwork. Maybe some spiritual guru can attain supreme bliss even in this, but I would say: Get out of such jobs. Don't fall victim to toxic positivity; don't force a silver lining onto everything; don't try to cover up your boredom and stress. Make preparations to move on from there in a search for joy.

The joy I experienced doing drama in college was actually a taste I had already sampled in school. In the eighth grade, I acted in a play. Even earlier, in childhood, I used to play games where we would assume different characters. We used to enact scenes from the 'Chandrakanta' serial. This is common among children; they play doctor-doctor, pretend to be teachers, pretend to be 'Shaktimaan'. But as time passes, these games fade away.

So should childhood dreams really be given much importance, when our exposure is so limited at that age? Maybe not, but even teenagers and young adults are conditioned by society. Everyone starts chasing one of the few popular careers - engineer, doctor, manager, lawyer, CA, teacher. So is it right to give preference to decisions made as adults, when they are less of our own choices and more of social conditioning? Which dreams should we really talk about then? The question arises: which dreams are truly our own? We circle right back to the topic of free will. But let's leave that for the next ebook.

For now, just think: have you ever felt joy somewhere - a joy that brings peace; have you ever found a fragrant dream; has something ever resonated within you? When that happens, it will pull you toward itself; you will feel a surge of energy inside. Reflect on whether you feel that *samvega* or not.

Chapter -9

On The Path Of Liberation

So far, we have discussed identifying your conditioning; seeking new exposure; trying many new things; immersing yourself in different types of work; searching for where true joy lies; and if you find that joy, it will generate a *samvega* within you; you'll start preparing on weekends.

For now, you've kept your resignation saved as a draft email; you open it and close it again. There's a restlessness to leave, but no urgency pushing you to arrive somewhere new.

Buddha left his home one night in pursuit of liberation, but you cannot bring yourself to send your resignation email at night to find your freedom. You say– "Abba nahi maanenge" (Father wouldn't agree).

But why should your father agree? That only happens in movies where the hero tearfully confesses his true feelings to his father, and the father gives his blessing. In real life, that's rare. Fathers have had their own exposure, which has not been too broad. If the father is a businessman, he doesn't stop his child from starting a business. But if he has always worked a job, then he believes that a job brings stability to life. Society consists of such fathers. The thinking of society is the thinking of the father. They don't know about being a fashion designer or a YouTuber. They don't personally know any successful musicians. So why would they agree to something they neither believe in nor understand?

The real question is, why do you even need their validation? Respecting your parents is one thing, but there's no sense in seeking their permission for everything, especially if you're over 18. If you think it's right, then go ahead and send that resignation email.

What will happen? They'll scold you? So, take the scolding. But if you let the fear of their scolding stop you from making decisions about your life, that's not a real excuse. This is just what you intend to use as an excuse; that's how it goes; nobody says, "I didn't have the courage." Everyone blames their parents for not letting them do something; otherwise, they claim, they would've achieved great things. It's just a way to hide your own fears. Your mind gets trapped in that very jail. You also want comfort, luxury, and a big car.

I never bought a car. Even though I could have purchased one with one or two years of easy installments. But I didn't. Even after changing jobs, I didn't get a car. I kept riding my motorcycle. First of all, I never had a taste for cars, bikes, sunglasses, shoes, or expensive phones. When there's so much joy to be found in reading, in acting, in writing poetry, why would I need all of that? Now, you might argue that if I weren't interested in a car, I could have at least bought a cheap one for convenience; after all, comfort does matter. That's true, but I wanted to save money. I wanted to get out. I wanted to be an artist.

My father kept supposing that I was under the influence of some friend, that I'd been affected by the college atmosphere. Whatever the influence, what difference does it make? Whether it's a childhood fantasy, someone's influence, or society's conditioning– what matters is that there was a fragrance to the dream. The dream had a *samvega*, and that *samvega* had its own truth. That ecstasy wasn't just a word– it was a feeling I'd experienced.

Maybe that feeling, that joy, that dream, that drive showed on my face. Maybe not to everyone, but perhaps to those who knew how to look. One day, when I was coming home on the office bus, a colleague I'd never met before came and sat by me. He worked at the same company, but I hadn't seen him before. He was on the bus only for that day because he had to go to a friend's place. He sat next to me. We introduced ourselves. He told me which department he worked in. Then, suddenly, he asked what I wanted to do. I was taken aback. I said I was in the supply chain department; it was going well.

He said, that's fine, but surely you want to do something outside of this job, right? I admitted that yes, I wanted to act, but I wondered how he knew. He replied, you just seem like you want to do something. In fact, he wanted the same.

At that time, he just wanted to buy a plot of land, though. He said he'd quit his job once he did so. I thought to myself– so you'll actually quit the job this way, will you? Even when I quit my job, he was still stuck there. But later, I found out he really had left. He was from Bihar. Some Bhojpuri films were being made in Mumbai, and he started acting in them.

Meeting him felt good. You should seek out people like yourself. These days, everyone talks about energy, vibration, manifestation, affirmation– all those things– it's all nonsense, pseudo-science. In my last ebook, "Power of the Universe," I discussed it in detail. But omitting all the supernatural stuff, if we look at it from a psychological perspective, a simple truth emerges– whatever you keep your mind occupied with, it ends up taking root in your mind.

In his poem, Pash wrote that history books lying on a shelf do not dream. I can't be sure about history books, but I can say for certain that people obsessed with increments, cost-of-living allowance, travel allowances, gossip about colleagues, cribbing about office work, or discussions about the latest car and phone models– such people don't have dreams. If you call the ambitions and desires of that rat race a dream, that's another matter– the dream of buying a Mercedes and the like. But if we're talking about dreams with some dreamlike element, those infused with wonder, those that make every nerve come alive– corporate slaves do not have such dreams.

I was working in the corporate world, but I didn't want to become a slave. Just as a person slowly gets sucked into quicksand, I didn't want to get trapped in that environment. One must be alert about this. Meeting a few people like yourself is a good reminder. And there should be some reminders of that infinite joy as well.

I used to ride in friends' cars; now I was travelling by flight, staying in big hotels, eating at expensive restaurants, all of which was fun, but pale in comparison to that joy. And that's because I'd already experienced that joy during my college days. The memory was still fresh in my mind. In a few years, it would fade like all memories. It would become just a story. No, I wouldn't let that happen. I wanted it, and I wanted it now, not at the age of sixty. I wanted it for a lifetime. But how would it happen? Should I just run off to Mumbai with a few bucks in my pocket? Yes, why not? My father could keep scolding me, but I wouldn't get caught by him. One day, I would escape from here. That's why I was saving money.

I thought I should taste that joy again. The conditions for quitting my job wouldn't arise for a little while yet. But why not do theatre even while staying here? Oh, but how would I make it to theatre rehearsals with a full-time job? It's not like my office was near ITO in Delhi, from where I could leave office at 5:30 and reach Mandi House at 6 for rehearsals. My office was in Gurgaon. I'd only get home by 7:30.

No matter. Instead of joining a theatre group, I would produce my own play. But where would I find other actors? Never mind, I'd do a solo play– a one-man show, where I'd be the only actor. Where would I get a script like that? After searching, I found a story by Edgar Allan Poe– The Tell-Tale Heart. In it, a man is so terrified by an old man's eye that he plans to murder him. Work began. I was the actor, the director, even the set designer. I named the play "The Vulture Eye." I rehearsed for many days. After the murder scene, I included a song, which a friend recorded and sent to me. Another friend designed the poster for the play. Where to perform it? I contacted various auditoriums in Delhi. Most were expensive, but finally, Alliance Française's auditorium on Lodhi Road was available for 5,000 rupees.

I didn't know anything about ticketing– putting shows on BookMyShow, handling taxes, and all that. So I just made entry passes for free admission. One weekend, I was roaming around Mandi House and Delhi University. There, I spoke to strangers, told them about the play, and handed passes to those who seemed interested. I told my friend and colleagues at the office too.

One day, I left work early and went to the auditorium, reviewed all their lights, created a lighting plan for the play, and handed it to my girlfriend: "Switch on this particular light at this line." My boss came with his family; a senior colleague was there as well. Friends came, my parents came, and two of my father's friends came as well.

The play dealt with multiple themes– authority, madness, crime, conscience, guilt. The beauty of intense art is that when you sit on the edge, you can feel profound emotions, provided the actor can create that resonance. And that happened. That same magic– meditation, hypnosis– the silence in the audience. It was a 55-minute play, and the audience was completely mesmerized.

My father and his friends enjoyed the play immensely. Though, for them, the most astonishing part was how someone could speak in English non-stop for 55 minutes without looking at a paper. Whatever the case, the play had such an impact on my father that the next day he said, "Your uncle told me– let him do what he wants. You were talking about acting college? Why not fill out an application form for one?"

That was a miracle. My father had agreed. Incredible! It had become a filmy story. I filled out application forms for the National School of Drama and the Film Institute in Pune. I started preparing. But soon enough, my father started saying again, "Forget it; why get involved in all this?" I said, "I've filled out the forms; I may as well take the exam."

This wasn't like the civil services exam, where everyone just fills out the forms anyway. Here, everyone who applied was extremely serious. There were only 20-25 seats, of which only 12-13 were general category seats. But my father kept insisting, "Forget this, there's nothing in it." I said, "This will make my way to Bollywood easier, otherwise if I just go to Mumbai without any educational training, it'll be too difficult."

Hearing this, my father got upset. He said that acting school was one thing, but wandering the streets of Mumbai like a vagabond - how could I even think of something like that? But why not? If a poet can't imagine something, who else will? Even if a poet is born in the middle class, he is a poet nonetheless.

Struggling in Mumbai is something even millions can think of, but a poet dares to imagine even going into exile. I packed my bag; said that the company was sending me for a plant visit for a few days. But a plant visit on a motorcycle? Yes, I'll leave the motorcycle at a friend's place and go to the airport from there.

Saying this, I set out for a friend's flat, who was pursuing his MBA in Gurgaon and staying there with other friends on rent. I'm talking about Vikram itself.

I went there for about two weeks. I got a bit emotional that, for the first time, I was leaving home by telling a lie, but soon realized that this wasn't something to get so emotional about. It was time to remove all distractions and prepare.

The first written round for the Pune Film Institute had gone pretty badly for me. I'd watched a lot of cinema, but didn't know that 'The Householder' was a 1963 Hindi movie, with Shashi Kapoor in the lead role. I mismatched several answers in the 'Match the Following' section. Still, there was some hope, because I'd written great answers for the subjective questions. That little hope turned into reality; I cleared the first round, and now it was time for the second round - the audition.

Vikram's flat was about 30-40 minutes from my office. As soon as I'd get back from work, I'd start rehearsing. For the National School of Drama audition, I selected a passage from Mohan Rakesh's play 'Lahron Ke Rajhans' (The Royal swans of the Waves). For the Pune Film Institute audition, I chose a passage from 'Wuthering Heights' - the one where Heathcliff fondly remembers Catherine. In the mountains, in the trees, amongst the people around him, he sees Catherine's face which laughs at him. As I performed this piece, tears escaped from the corners of my eyes.

Even today, remembering it sends shivers all over me. In real life, we often wear a shield of ego. The things we need to say, we don't. We hesitate, suppress, hide. We clamp down our feelings, telling ourselves that nothing affects us. In defending our ego, we emotionally detach ourselves. Life becomes a play, and look how sometimes a play brings us alive. Through a character, we feel everything, express it, touching the innermost layers of emotion. Yes, it was a kind of catharsis. I was shaken to my core.

The jury members asked me to sit down. They gave me a couple of moments to compose myself, then asked a few questions. I recited a poem for them about riots and disturbances.

Tell me, which God do you worship, O preacher!
The God who won, or the one who lost?

Whom you search for in temple-mosque 'Gulfam',
Someone killed Him in the riots yesterday.

The jury loved this poem. I was confident I would clear this round, and I did.

The third round was a five-day workshop. I went to Pune for it. One of those jury members was here too. He recognized me and said, "Wow, what a poem you had recited; I want everyone to hear it." So I recited it, but one guest member didn't like it. He said, "Why do you use such heavy Urdu words? My father wrote in Hindustani; you should write in Hindustani too."

I should've replied, "Okay, sir," but instead I said, "Sir, sometimes I write poetry in pure Hindi, sometimes in English, sometimes in Urdu, and sometimes in Hindustani. Poetry chooses its own words."

My response was taken as an argument. The group coordinator gestured from behind for me to keep quiet, so I did. This same group coordinator turned out to be a curse for our group. Sixty people were selected for this round, divided into three groups of twenty each. The group coordinator would give us activities, and as soon as we did anything, he'd start cursing us. Hahaha. I already felt the ship was sinking. Five days later, the final result was announced, and it was obvious: from the other forty, twenty-one got selected, while from our group of twenty, only two.

Anyway, it's fine. Maybe I should have prepared more. I didn't get selected in the National School of Drama either. They asked me to sing something, and I sang horribly out of tune; I can't sing. I thought, "Okay, next year then." Then I felt, "No, not next year." I was always in a hurry. I decided I would go to Mumbai.

But now, what would I tell my father? My mother always stood by my dreams. She used to say, "Whatever you do, you'll do well." But for my father, only the IAS was acceptable. Somehow, one day he said, "Okay, check out the acting college." But now, he'd say, "See, I gave you permission to open a little window to your dreams, but now that you haven't been selected, just go back to your job and don't even think about becoming a vagabond."

Fine. I just won't say anything. My brother and I decided we wouldn't even tell dad about not getting selected; we'd just lie that I got through. Because if I told the truth, there would be a fight - one that wouldn't last for a couple of days. Dad would keep asking every three days if I got any film roles yet. The struggle in the city of dreams is a mountain in itself; I couldn't handle his stress along with mine. So I resolved to quietly leave my job and reach Mumbai in two-three months.

Meanwhile, I'd broken up with my girlfriend. Reasons? Never mind.

I started talking to another girl on social media. She told me she'd loved me for eight years; she had never thought of anyone else, but could never tell me. Oh, such madness! And look how I had been hanging about in the wrong place. We started talking on the phone. I began dreaming about what our house would look like. She was studying law in another city. We'd been talking for almost two months when she was coming home for the holidays. My heart was pounding.

I took a 'cool' shirt in my office bag. I changed into it at lunch, got on my bike, and went to the airport to receive her, with chocolates and flowers. I told her then that I was quitting my job. She said, "Okay, my parents should be here soon; you should go." I left, smiling.

That smile vanished quickly when she didn't pick up her phone the next day or respond to any messages. I kept messaging, asking her to just tell me what happened. She finally said, "That's it, you and I are done. My parents will never accept someone who's quitting his job."

I said, "If even my own father can't accept my leaving the job, what can I expect from your father? Tell me about yourself– what do you want?" She replied, "I can't go against my parents." So was that it? All that passion of eight years?

Well, just as people blame parents for not following their dreams, they could use them as an excuse to leave a romance too. She was running her own prison race. She ran fast, landed a top job, and married a wealthy businessman. Good that there was no confusion in her mind. Had she made some excuse to break up after a while, it would've been worse; better that she told me clearly now.

Did I lose love because I chased my dreams? No. On the contrary, it scares me to think what would have happened if I hadn't planned to quit my job; maybe neither of us would've realized how hollow her "mad love" was, and I would have ended up marrying her. Better that things are clear now.

Am I now going to become a superstar for revenge, just to show her? In movies and Insta reels, you often see this: the guy becomes a superstar, very rich, and only then does the girl realize his worth. People say success is the best revenge. I have no such foolish obsessions. I don't carry the burden of having to prove anything to anyone, or of having to make my parents proud. If someone wants their name to shine, they can just put a light on their nameplate. What I do, I do for myself. Whoever can be a part of this happiness, that's great.

My boss was part of my happiness. I wasn't a superstar yet, but just chasing your dreams is happiness enough, if you can feel it. I submitted my notice at the office. I told my boss the truth, that I was going to Mumbai. Half the world knew the real reason, meaning those who were close to me. The other half believed I was going to film school, meaning those who were close to my parents. Let the lie spread; if it's uncovered someday, so be it– no big deal! People will judge and say I'm a big liar. Hahaha, let them. I'll tell everyone myself that I escaped prison on the sly. I'm saying it openly for the first time today.

These aren't just personal stories. They are mine, yours, and those of all of us. These things need to be talked about, or how else can people escape their prisons and leave their jobs? How would the city of dreams bloom?

Chapter -10

The Adventures of Vijeta Dahiya

There was a huge crowd in the city of dreams. The good thing was that my brother was already working in Mumbai at that time, so I had a place to stay. Moreover, it was in Navi Mumbai, which, unlike the rest of Mumbai, wasn't a crowded area. There was a mountain in Belapur with a temple atop it. Sometimes I would ride my bike there, carrying my camera.

I had bought a new camera. Even after that, I had a decent amount of money left in my account. If needed, I could've picked up a job in Mumbai, which would allow me to attend auditions in the evenings and on weekends. But for the time being, there was no need. At that moment, I was writing a feature film script– 'Ek Thi Maya.' I was also reading books and going to auditions.

Before coming to Mumbai, I thought I'd just go straight to auditions, perform, and land a good role. It seemed like a straightforward affair. But that wasn't the case. The main characters were already cast beforehand. Auditions were for roles where you'd just be a face in the crowd, with no dialogue, appearing in the frame for barely ten seconds– or for biscuit, chocolate, and similar commercials.

There were no dialogues, yet in the audition, you'd be asked to recite half a page of script. Anyway, I went through it, but there was another problem. If the audition line grew too long, someone would come from inside and do a mass elimination right on the spot. You wait, you wait, you leave, you too, you wait. Often, I was among those told to leave. I used to wonder in surprise: I came after seeing all the conditions on the casting call poster– age, height, everything; what is it in my face that makes them think I'm not suitable for a biscuit ad? What's wrong with my face that people wouldn't want to eat chocolate after seeing me eat it?

A friend gave such an explanation that it warmed my heart. He said my face looks like a hero's; if I'm on the side, people wouldn't even look at the hero. It was a comforting thought.

This friend said another thing– something many people had already told me. Everyone would say it as if it were a big secret, known only to them, and they were divulging it for my benefit. They would whisper in a hushed tone that in the film industry, contacts matter; it's all about networking– build your contacts. Now, I thought to myself, I would love to build contacts, but no one wants to make contact with me; I'm just a struggling actor. Still, I kept going to the Prithvi Theatre. I kept trying.

All of this felt strange, like that couplet by Majrooh Sultanpuri –

> We're like the wares of the street and market,
> Every gaze lingers on us, as if we are for sale.

> हम हैं मता-ए-कूचा-ओ-बाज़ार की तरह
> उठती है हर निगाह ख़रीदार की तरह

Then I joined a famous theatre group, whose shows I'd watched before. I asked one of the group members; he asked the director, then came back to tell me it was fine– come for rehearsals. The director didn't even bother to have an introduction, nor did the other group members. It felt odd, but I just went and sat on the side, watching the rehearsal. Then I was assigned to assist someone with photocopying.

One morning, they had me washing teacups. I had no problem washing cups, but there was no role, no learning involved. I hadn't joined a theatre group just to wash cups. I could wash cups at home as well. The boy assisting me had been doing just that for a year. Another boy got a small role in a play, but only after two years.

This wasn't going to work. I tried to increase my participation, to come to the director's notice. But the director didn't even bother replying to a "good evening." I wrote something on paper about one of his plays– like a thoughtful analysis, reading which he'd feel I was a creative person. But he just sent word through one of his actors– go home, and that they would call me for backstage work on the day of the show.

I'd analyzed his play, so a creative discussion should have taken place. But what happened instead? He treated me like an outcaste. Then, on the day of the show, the assistant called, asking me to come for backstage work. I told him to go to hell– not exactly in those words, but that was the sentiment. Why should I go just to do backstage for a day?

"I simply came to Mumbai with a couple of bucks in my pocket"– this line is great for bragging in celebrity interviews. But in reality, it's better to take a few days off work and get a sense of the field first. It's good to plan in advance. But remember, no matter how much you plan, as soon as you hit the ground, something or the other will go wrong. You can't plan for everything. But some planning can help.

Auditions were for crappy roles, and on top of that, the films themselves were so lousy. I felt like– what's even the point of being seen once on the big screen? Having read literature since childhood, having watched world cinema, I had an urge to do something of quality, to do a good role in a good film. But landing even a small role was tough, dreaming of acting in a film of my own choice– it was laughable.

Amidst all this, my brother suggested I should learn filmmaking. He said, "As a kid, you don't understand direction; you just see actors on the screen, so you only dream of acting. But you talk about films with such passion; your mind is creative; you write by imagining the whole picture. Make your own film, then act in it yourself."

I felt he was right. That's why I bought a handycam. I joined a workshop that had about seven or eight classes, which would give me a basic understanding of filmmaking. I made a three-minute film; shot and edited it myself. It was simply about someone's bike getting a puncture; he takes it to the repairman, and the guy fixes it. This was assigned to learn about continuity. I named the film *'Tyre Tyre Phish.'*

There were just seven or eight of us in the film workshop, and it was held on weekends in some college classroom in Mumbai. The friends in the workshop admired the film.

Now comes the realization that in Mumbai, everything is rented. How would I make films here? Maybe I should just go back. In Delhi-Haryana, I had my home, village, family, relatives, and friends. Satyajit Ray made his first film similarly.

At the same time, my brother was planning to move to Delhi; he got a job there and returned home. But how could I go home? I'd told everyone I was at the Pune Film Institute.

So I rented a flat a few kilometers away from home and went back into hiding. My brother often came to meet me in the evening. Sometimes there would be partying with friends. Back then, I didn't know how to cook much. Should I hire someone to cook? It felt like too much expense, plus buying flour, lentils, rice, and vegetables seemed like a hassle. So I ate at cheap roadside dhabas.

One day, there was a wedding tent set up near my flat. Instead of eating at the dhaba, I decided to eat at the wedding. I was serving myself some shahi paneer when I heard a voice from behind: "Vijeta". My hands froze. I turned to see my aunt. She asked how I was, then inquired if my parents had also come.

Actually, I had gatecrashed just a random wedding, but later found out that the family sort of knew us. So my aunt assumed I had come by invitation. I replied that my parents hadn't come; I was there with a friend. She asked how my film course in Pune was going. I told her everything was great, I was in Delhi for just two days.

A few days later, she mentioned it to my mother on the phone. My mother called me, asked if I'd come to Delhi. I made up an excuse that I had a two-day shoot in Delhi; we were in a hurry, so just stopped by the wedding for food, then had to rush to catch the flight; hence, I couldn't come home. I figured then that it was better to just eat at the dhaba.

The road in front of my flat was dug up. Sometimes the motor wouldn't pump water, so I'd call the plumber. On such occasions, I would have to get by on very little water the whole day. I lived a very frugal life. Looking back, it feels like that was a really struggling time, but don't get emotional– I was not that troubled, actually. It was a very creative period.

During that time, I spent a month writing my first feature-film script, '*Dararein*'. I read novels; wrote stories and poems.

When I needed money, I ventured:

- I started teaching part-time at a coaching centre.
- I conducted a theatre workshop for school children and got the younger kids to stage a play on 'The Wizard of Oz' while the older ones performed 'A Christmas Carol' by Charles Dickens.
- Once, I helped college students put together a play, 'Haraị Gulab' (The Green Rose), for their cultural fest.

- An NGO needed a street play to represent themselves at the Himachal government's Health Fair. I gathered people and went to perform a street play. I had never imagined you could earn money even from theatre which is seen as such a humble medium.
- Then I ran a 5-day filmmaking workshop for volunteers of an NGO in Jodhpur, so they could make documentaries.
- A documentary maker from South Korea was there to shoot a documentary on child marriage. I assisted him. Later, that documentary was shown on a South Korean TV channel. People there watched me on TV.

That's how I survived. During this period, I also started talking to another girl on Facebook. One of her friends happened to be from my neighboring area. She had told her about me, that I'd studied at Delhi College of Engineering and was now at film school. She found me on Facebook. She didn't mention that she knew about me from somewhere. She said, you write poetry on Facebook; that's why I wanted to talk. We chatted on Messenger, then started talking on the phone.

I don't lie without reason. So I told her I'd quit my job. I had told my parents that I was going to Pune Film Institute. But I had gone to Mumbai, and after returning from there, now I was trying to make my own film. She said – hats off to you; how can someone be so crazy for their dreams as to leave a comfortable life and live like this. Someone had rejected me once for this same thing, which now left someone else enamored. We fell in love.

Two years later, we got married. As I write this, she's sitting next to me sipping coffee.

At that time, after having finished writing the script for '*Dararein*', I started casting for the film. I realized that doing camera work plus acting would be tough. So, it was better to let others act in this one. I put up casting-call posters in colleges in Delhi and Rohtak. People came for auditions.

I kept three rounds in the audition– acting, movement, and the capacity to listen and understand. If the actors got stuck, I'd give them more chances. I would explain where they were going wrong, tell them to correct it, and try again. That's how the actors were selected.

Then one day, the lead actor ran away. He was enrolled in a course at an acting institute in Chandigarh. So it was clear that he was serious about acting. But for some reason, he suddenly refused.

Then I found another one. But after some time, he said he wanted to run for councillor, and the people investing in him told him that acting would damage his serious image. So, he left too.

I could have found a third actor for the role, but gathering the rest of the cast, locations, props– everything became difficult, because among my parents, relatives, and their entire circle, the word was that I was at the Film Institute in Pune.

It felt like simply surviving wouldn't cut it. Even to make a low-budget film, you need some budget. I had to start earning decently again. At that time, I had no business ideas. I didn't know much about getting into the media. I filled out the form for a government job– the Combined Graduate Level Exam (CGLE). Even when I took the prelims, I still wasn't sure if I actually wanted to take the exam; so I hadn't prepared at all. Still, I cleared the prelims. Being good at studies always proves useful in some way or another.

One day at home, I finally told everyone everything. For my father, it was shocking. But what helped absorb this shock was the fact that I had cleared the prelims for a government job. It was also surprising for him that someone like me would consider a government job. Then I spent the next four months preparing for the mains exam and went for the interview. I had checked the answers afterward, and it was clear that I'd be selected.

Now, for a week, I stayed with a Swang troupe in Haryana. They were staying at the choupal of a village near Gohana. The performance took place in the evenings. For the first time, I played a small role in a Saang performance.

Right at that time, the results were declared, and I found out that I had been selected for the government job. Lakhs of people take this exam. I ranked 357. There was a gap of 7–8 months before joining.

My brother had done an M.A. in Social Work. He started a project. There were many girls and women in the rural areas of Delhi who couldn't go to the city for coaching, and because of that, they couldn't find employment. The result was that their social status never improved. So, the idea was to provide free coaching for the primary teacher recruitment exam right at a village choupal. Word spread, and 80 girls from nearby villages started coming there to study. My brother taught general knowledge and educational psychology. I taught math and English.

The coaching went on for two months. Out of those, 15–16 girls were selected as primary teachers. A few more got selected the next year. On August 15th, my brother and I had our photos published in a newspaper.

Then there came a project with an NGO to perform a street play in 15 schools and colleges across Haryana. My brother wrote the play– "Jamoore Ka Byah" (The Sidekick's Wedding). He played the role of Jamura, and I played Ustaad. In some performances, we switched roles. There were six of us– the actors– one of whom was my new girlfriend. Wherever we performed, all the teachers and students praised us.

But at a college in Sonipat, there were some very rowdy students who just wanted to hoot. Even then, we kept the play going. In a street play, the actors' energy makes a big difference. In the end, we managed to engage even those boys; they clapped too.

One boy came up to me and said, "Please forgive us, we created a lot of chaos, but you didn't stop, and you actually managed to silence us; this play truly opened my eyes today; now I'll treat every girl better."

That was a huge compliment for us, that a stranger would come up on his own and say something like that. I wondered whether a play or a film is enough to change someone's outlook. I think that question comes later; first, artists should at least try to create such powerful art.

Nowadays, everything seems to be lost in the clamour of "what will work."

There was a surge rising in my heart that, if not '*Dararein*', then at least something should be made. If not a feature film, then a short film. My brother and I were eating at Aggarwal Sweets nearby. An old woman came into the shop and asked for golgappas. That cost ₹15 a plate. She said she only had ten rupees but really wanted to eat. The shopkeeper, either out of sympathy or as a customer-retention policy, whatever the reason, gave her the golgappa token for ten rupees. We watched this. We wondered, what if he hadn't given her the token? If that poor old woman left with a heavy heart and then had an accident on the road, how guilty would the shopkeeper feel! Would her spirit haunt him?

That sparked the idea for my short film '*Ek Plate Chowmein*' (A Plate of Chowmein). I quickly wrote the script. I already had a handycam. I even bought a bluetooth mic for it. My brother played the shopkeeper; by then, he was married, and my sister-in-law played the shopkeeper's wife. I persuaded my mother to play the old woman.

I told the owner of Aggarwal Sweets that we would shoot there for a day. He was also a man of revolutionary thoughts like us, would read poetry, and we always had good conversations. He said there was no need to ask; the shop is yours, shoot whenever you want.

But how to shoot at home? My father would create a ruckus. All the scenes at home were night scenes, and my father would always be there at night. We put up curtains and newspapers on the windows to turn day into night. I had to shoot at my own home stealthily.

How to show the car accident scene? I had only very basic editing knowledge; I didn't know anything about VFX. So, I learned it from YouTube. I put the camera on a tripod and first shot the actor crossing the road. Then, from exactly the same camera position, I shot the car passing. Then I overlapped both footages in the editing software, tweaking things around. The editing software was a trial version. The whole film was put together this way, through makeshift techniques.

People liked the film for the story. Otherwise, there were a lot of flaws in the film's look and the sound too. I got the chance to learn from this, so that such mistakes wouldn't happen while making *'Dararein'*. I started watching YouTube videos to better understand filmmaking. I understood the importance of lighting. Of course, I kept watching films too.

But then the time arrived to join the government job.

□□

Chapter - 11

The Fire Must Keep Burning

I got posted as an Assistant Section Officer in the Ministry of External Affairs.

Two months after this, I got married. It was a simple affair. I took no dowry; no lavish 25–30 lakh rupee wedding; neither lehenga of one lakh nor sherwani of fifty thousand. I wore a dhoti-kurta. My wife had seen Anushka Sharma in a movie wearing a specific lehenga, so she took that photo to a local boutique and had one made just like it. In a government community hall, all the ceremonies and rituals were done in the presence of close ones. The priest from our apartment conducted all of this. Our family's traditional caterer got healthy and tasty food prepared in pure desi ghee. By about 6–7 pm, the wedding was done. The farewell happened on the same motorcycle I used to ride at that time.

The next evening, we had a party with friends. My wife got a gown designed for that day, and I wore a coat-pant. There were our friends from school and college, my former boss in Ranbaxy, and new friends from the Ministry of External Affairs came too.

Our entry was on a camel. There was a screening of my short film "Ek plate chowmein." There was food, drinks, dancing, conversations, laughter. There was no stage set up that day because my wife and I wanted to roam around and enjoy instead of posing on the stage. If anyone wanted to take a photo, they could just come up to us. We had told the photographer that the wedding wasn't for the camera, rather the camera was there for the wedding. So, don't tell anyone to pose. Stay in the background and click natural photos.

The atmosphere at the new government office was very 'government-like.' There's a joke in the newspaper for kids: The teacher asks, what is 'sarkar' (government)? The student says, "sarak sarak ke chalne wali car ko sarkar kehte hain," i.e. the government is like a car that moves slowly. This joke tells a harsh truth. You must also imagine government jobs as people sitting on chairs, lost in paperwork, with repetitive tasks. If you think this, you're right. That's what it was.

I tried to work smartly. I shifted template-type work to Microsoft Excel, so that the repetitive work that required around an hour could now be done in 5 min, and with much more accuracy. Tasks that would involve three months of correspondence, letters going back and forth, I started using the office phone effectively. I would call the number given on the letter, discuss the matter, and then sent a final letter.

Many people in government jobs have a mantra- "Bane raho pagla, kaam karega agla" (Keep acting dumb, and someone else will do the work). That 'someone else' was me. But I always felt it's better to work sincerely. First, because that's what you're paid for, and second, if you have to go to the office and work anyway, you might as well do it diligently.

There were rewards for this diligence. One reward was more work, and the other was that if you ever asked for leave, it was hard to get one, since so much now depended on you. The boss was kind of grumpy and was used to his old ways. If I started reading a novel on finishing my work, he would object to that too.

However, my boss's boss and those even higher up - the Deputy Secretary and Joint Secretary - praised me a lot. Once, the Joint Secretary said, "What are you doing here? Your level is far above this work. If you want to stay in a government job, why don't you clear the Civil Services Exam and join in Class-I?" I told him about my being an artist. I told him about 'Ek plate chowmein.'

I also found out that there was another Joint Secretary whose novel 'Q & A' was made into a film by Danny Boyle - 'Slumdog Millionaire' - which won 8 Oscars. It felt good to know that there were a few people from my artistic tribe here as well. During training, I learned the rules about how you could do creative work on the side. If there were no money involved, it was just like any other hobby. But even if it involved money, you could still do some creative work, provided it didn't become a regular source of income.

Every September, there used to be a Hindi Fortnight (Pakhwada) event focused around Hindi Diwas, which had poetry competitions, essay competitions, debates, and other events. I used to participate in those and win prizes. Once, I even received a certificate from External Affairs Minister Sushma Swaraj. In these events, I met some other creative people like myself, who became friends. Sometimes they would recite their poems to me, and sometimes I would tell them my stories.

Besides these creative friends, I was also part of a 'desi club' of 5–6 friends. Many times, I would have lunch with them, or sometimes have evening tea. These people were always joking and laughing, and they were like a shield for me, protecting me from the government office environment.

People may work in the Ministry of External Affairs, but they had no interest in India's foreign policy. Discussions about society and politics were useless to them. They viewed cinema and music just as means to kill time. Literature, poetry, theatre, painting, philosophy– they didn't even want to hear about them. There was a museum outside the office building, but in years of service, not once had they bothered to visit it. Even about their own work, there was little enthusiasm. Their conversations centered around complaints about their boss and their department colleagues.

Many section officers had been promoted from clerk positions after twenty years. Several of them didn't know how to work. They were always flustered. And in many sections, it was also true that there was a lazy guy who acted dumb, and the work had to be done by others. So, to be honest, sometimes their complaints were justified, but how many times can you have the same conversation? After that, their topic of discussion shifted to DA (dearness allowance), travel allowance, increments, pay commissions, and pensions.

Once, during lunch, it occurred to me that Pranab Mukherjee served in South Block (External Affairs Minister), then in the opposing North Block (Finance Minister). He should have come here (PMO), but instead went over there (Rashtrapati Bhavan). A colleague, engrossed in the government office ambience, quickly said, "It turned out great for him." I started wondering. A man who could have become Prime Minister was made President; how is that great? Normally, anyone would prefer to be the Prime Minister over the President. I wondered if there was a deeper meaning in his words. I asked, and he answered, "As Prime Minister, you have all the hassles in the world; as President, you get to travel abroad on government expense and collect your DA and TA. Life is good."

Damn! I'd never thought that DA and TA were the ultimate truths of life. I folded my hands before his wisdom.

There needs to be a change in the recruitment process of government jobs; a common exam is fine for clerks, but the common exam for Class-1 and Class-2 jobs should be stopped. Each ministry should advertise its own vacancies. Those in the Ministry of Culture should have an interest in culture. Those in the Ministry of External Affairs should know the geography, history, and politics of different countries; they should understand diplomacy. In the Postal Department, there should be people who find beauty in letter writing. IPS officers should be those who know something about law. The government process should be made efficient.

Currently, if someone does no work, there is no punishment for delay; but if someone makes a mistake, there's punishment– this should change. This way, every government department would develop some dynamism and this government office environment would change. The connotation attached to the word 'governmental' would change.

But for now, my concern was that this government environment might end up changing me. Of those who joined with me, many were smart, hardworking, and honest people, but were steadily becoming typical government personnel. The same thing from the movie *'Taxi Driver'*– a man becomes his job. I had to safeguard myself. I had to keep my inner artist alive.

That's why, first, I stuck with my creative friends; second, with the desi club; and third, with myself. I'd gotten over the awkward feeling of wandering alone, of the hesitation that someone might question why I was alone– way back in school. In school, college, my first job, and now here too, I often roamed alone. I always had friends as well; I would hang out with them and have fun, but I also enjoyed wandering alone.

Since childhood, there was always something running through my mind, which I did not even want to stop. There was a depth and a joy in it. Then, in the Hindi syllabus, I read a lesson, *'Himmat Aur Zindagi'* (Courage and Life), where Dinkar says:

"A courageous man enjoys even those dreams which have no practical meaning. A courageous man does not borrow dreams; he is immersed in his own thoughts and reads his own book. To walk and graze in a herd is the work of buffaloes and sheep. A lion, even when utterly alone, is happily engrossed."

Reading this gave me great comfort, as if someone had understood me so well.

What I always felt was that, look, friend, we've talked, we've had fun, but after that, if

- you can tell something interesting, like an anecdote from your childhood, or
- you want to share something personal, or
- a wonderful thought has emerged in your mind, or
- you can make me cry or laugh,

then go ahead and tell me.

Otherwise, if you want to do small talk to fill the silence by saying it's very hot these days, then you'd better leave that time for me. In the mornings, when going to the office or coming back, I'd travel alone; otherwise, it would just feel like an extension of office hours. I'd even go alone to the canteen for tea. There, I'd think about how to make a film.

Chapter -12

I Made a Film

Then one day, I started to make a film. *'Dararein'* is the story of three brothers. For the youngest brother's role, two people had already dropped out, so this time I decided to do it myself. My wife played the role of the youngest brother's wife. My brother and sister-in-law played the middle brother and his wife. So four roles were covered within our family.

For the eldest brother's role, I cast a folk raagini singer from Haryana who lived nearby. For the eldest sister-in-law's role, I went for a sister-in-law from our extended family.

As for the camera? I had my handycam. My father joked, "What kind of film can you make with such a small camera?" I said, "Doesn't matter, we'll make something. We'll release it in Haryana's CD circuit. For that, this is fine."

Lights? I got a bulb holder fitted with a long wire, and bought two CFL lights normally used at home. Looking back now, I can see this was a bad decision because a film is never truly zero-budget. Certainly not a feature film. So even if your budget is low, you should spend about 15,000 rupees and buy a 5-in-1 reflector, two LED video lights, two softboxes, and two light stands.

But the truth is, I did zero budgeting. My plan was to spend money only when absolutely necessary, when something really couldn't be done without, and at the end, I would see the total expense.

For sound, there was the same camera-attached bluetooth mic that I had used for 'Ek plate chowmein'. That too was foolish. To be honest, the film workshop had made a passing mention about dubbing systems and on-location sync sound. I realized only later that even in sync sound, only the dialogue is recorded, and you can't use this kind of Bluetooth mic for that.

Now I also understand that for the price I paid for the handycam, ₹60,000, I could have bought a cheap DSLR and two lenses.

In one film workshop class, we were taught the history of cinema. I'm not saying that's unimportant, but that theory you can read on your own. If there had been a class about low-budget film production, it would have been much better.

Anyway, I had set my boat afloat in the river. Now, whatever rapids would come midstream, I'd face them. I didn't have to wait long. On the very first day of the shoot, we began with a simple scene. But the eldest sister-in-law just couldn't act. The problem wasn't that her acting was bad, but she was so shy and hesitant that she just couldn't open up. The woman playing the neighbour's role volunteered, "I'll take on the eldest sister-in-law's main role." I agreed. She did it very well, even though she was a wrestler and acting for the first time. On the first day, we finished two scenes. But on the second day, the actor playing the eldest brother dropped out despite having done well the previous day. Now he felt it was too big a commitment. After just two days of shooting, the film was stalled again.

So began another search for the role of the eldest brother. My brother knew a senior lawyer who had always felt the urge to act since his youth. When we were starting the film, my brother told him about it and he came for an audition. He too was hesitant; whenever he delivered a dialogue, a smile would break out on his face. We had rejected him initially, casting the raagini singer instead. Now my brother suggested we give him another try. Even if he scored less on the acting part, we could help him improve; what we needed more was commitment. We needed an actor with real passion, so he wouldn't run away midway. So, we called him again, for another audition, and finalized the role for him. Two months had already passed. The shoot resumed.

The main location was my sister-in-law's parents' house, which in the film was shown as the home of the eldest and middle brothers. Another location was our own flat, which in the film became the youngest brother's house. There were also flashback scenes showing the three brothers living together twenty years ago. For that, we used an aunt's village house, in the backyard area. The remaining locations were outdoor ones– a temple, a small canal, fields, a wrestling ground, a bike showroom, a jeweller's shop, a barber's shop, etc. These locations had only one or two scenes each; just a day's shoot; so no major issues. Just as I'd thought on my return from Mumbai, Delhi–Haryana is my home turf; I'd get locations and actors; and that had turned out to be true.

The poor actors would first perform their scenes. When they didn't have any scenes, they'd hold up the lights. Everyone's life was being enriched by an unforgettable chapter– one they'd remember until the end of their lives.

We shot on the weekends for over a year and a half. I was the one handling the camera. When it was my scene, I'd ask a friend to stand at my mark, frame the shot, and then my friend would operate the camera. He supported me selflessly.

There weren't just tripod-based static shots, but also some tracking shots. For those, we had no crane or slider. It was a test of our balancing skills. A few of my scenes were on a scooter, and one on a jeep. Some scenes were of the eldest brother riding his bicycle. For these, one of us would ride a motorcycle, someone else would sit facing backward holding the camera, and shoot. Sometimes it was me, and at other times, my brother or my friend.

So many problems arose– a whole book could be written about them. Sometimes, the parents of a child actor would suddenly refuse to continue, saying their hobby was satisfied and no more days would be allowed. We'd have to request them, "Just one last day." Then, rushing around, we'd film all their scenes at once. Sometimes, in the fields, the camera's battery would die. That was my foolishness, of not buying an extra battery, even though it wasn't all that expensive. Sometimes it rained every weekend for four to five weeks straight.

But there was neither any strict shooting schedule nor the pressure of a producer. So, though we'd get tired at times, there was never much stress on the mind. Shooting was fun. There was always laughter and jokes between the shots.

I'd save the footage to the laptop and watch it, finding joy in it. The film workshop teacher had once said: a filmmaker is a kind of god; they create their own world. These moments felt just like that– a tickle inside, marvelling at your own creation.

I'd go alone, riding my bike, to scout the next location– that too was enjoyable. And the most amazing feeling was watching an actor through the camera, and when they performed so well that you'd forget everything around you, including calling "cut." An absolutely marvellous feeling. Resonance.

It felt like the film was turning out well. Gradually, a desire for perfection crept in; at the very least, the acting had to be extraordinary. Once, there was a critical scene's final shot. It took 78 retakes from 2 PM until 9 at night.

After the film had been shot, it was time to edit. While I had also edited "*Ek plate chowmein*," that was a drama-horror film, entirely story-based, driven by 'what happens next.' But '*Dararein*' was a deeper film, driven by emotions. Each scene offered many editing choices. The younger brother is riding away in a car, the eldest brother following on a bicycle– how long should this shot last? 5 seconds? 25 seconds? Or 55 seconds?

There were several such scenes with just background score, no dialogue. There were two songs in the film, both in the background. Even the scenes with dialogue often weren't snappy; the pauses between lines - how long should they be? One second? One second and ten frames? Two seconds?

I realized this wasn't going to be easy. Was I ready for it? Maybe not. So, I bought two books on editing. One was In the Blink of an Eye, the famous book by legendary Hollywood editor Walter Murch, where he outlines six factors for making editing cuts. The second book was Fine Cuts: The Art of European Film Editing, in which editors who have worked on films by great directors like Ingmar Bergman and François Truffaut shared their own editing processes.

I'd read these books on the metro on my way to and from the office. After finishing my work at the office, if I had any time left, instead of going out, I'd read. After reading both books, my confidence grew. I understood the basics: that you have to gauge the rhythm of a scene and keep the editing in sync with that rhythm, and that you shouldn't make forced edit cuts without motivation.

Film editing is more creative than technical. The technical part of operating the editing software– I learned that from YouTube.

Meanwhile, I'd also applied to the Satyajit Ray Film & TV Institute (SRFTI), Kolkata, for the direction and cinematography courses. There was a written test first. I was shortlisted for the cinematography course. The next round was a five-day workshop on campus. My All-India rank was 9, but only 8 would be admitted. I was first on the waiting list, but the waiting list never cleared.

I applied again for the cinematography course. The shoot for *Dararein* had started by then. In the interview, I showed them some footage. One board member said, "You already know how to do such amazing work– what will you even learn here?" I thought he was just teasing me. I said, "No sir, I want to learn."

When the result came out, this time my rank was 4th. I was selected. But suddenly my mind changed. By then, I was married, and I didn't want to leave my wife or my family for so many years.

During the workshop, I spent five days in the hostel. I found out that although it was a three-year course, it often stretches up to five years. Then you go to Mumbai. You work as an assistant for several years. If you're very talented, like Santosh Sivan, you might become a chief cinematographer in eight to nine years, and then direct your own film five years after that– so about twenty years from now.

It seemed fine keeping a career in mind; you'd start earning. But I didn't want a career. I wanted to make movies– right now. First *Dararein,* then other films. I didn't go; I kept working at my job.

But for how long would the job continue? That question began to haunt me. Once, I was leaving for the office with my brother. By then, he had finished law school and was practicing. He had to go to his court that day, and I had my office. Suddenly, we decided, forget it; let's take the day off. I called the office and took leave. We drove the car toward the village fields instead. We discussed our lives.

We realized there would never be an 'auspicious' time to quit a job. Before the government-office atmosphere completely sucked me into it, I needed to move out. I shared this thought with my wife and my sister-in-law. They both said, "If it feels right, quit! You have our full support."

Two days later, I resigned. People had heard of someone quitting to join another government job, or in rare cases, to join an MBA program. But this kind of resignation– no one had seen or heard of before. It was so shocking to everyone that the Minister of State for External Affairs called me into his office, saying, "Why are you quitting?" I said, "Sir, I am an artist; I have some dreams." He asked sympathetically, "Can't you pursue that while working here? Tell me honestly– are you being harassed? Is the workload too much? If you want, I can change your section right now."

I said, "No sir, nothing of the sort. I've always done my job well here. But now I want to do something creative; something with my own unique mark." He told me, "All the best."

I wanted to share this with the Joint Secretary of my former department as well. I went to his office and told him I was quitting. He said, "Vijeta, why did it take you so long? Good that you're finally leaving; you'll do something remarkable."

A friend from the desi club heard about it. He came to meet me, very worried, saying, "The film line is so risky; quitting your job like this isn't wise. Still, if you're adamant, take a leave without pay for as long as you need. If nothing works out, you'll have a way back." Most others gave me the same advice. But I'd decided that if I couldn't do my most favourite work, then I'd do my next favourite. After so much education and intelligence, I shouldn't be afraid of making ends meet. So I gave a full and final resignation.

I met each of my office friends, one by one, had parties, and finally, after the notice period ended, I left. That day, I had lunch with my brother and some friends at a restaurant nearby.

Some payments from the office, like group insurance money, still hadn't been cleared. I called 3–4 times, but it was the usual government runaround: "We'll do it today, we'll do it tomorrow." Would I have to go to the office to get this cleared? I'd seen retired employees running after such thing. But no, I wasn't going to do that. It was just 5–6 thousand rupees. I decided to let it go and focus ahead.

My parents didn't know I'd quit. So, I would leave home in the morning and then go to a friend's place who was living in a hostel, preparing for a government job. I'd sit there and edit on my laptop.

The film's music was being composed by a music composer. I'd made a video for one of his songs, and in return, he was now composing music for my film. He'd made the tune so difficult that it was hard to find a singer in Haryana who could sing it. After searching a lot, we found one male and one female singer, both of whom were trained in classical music. We called the singers and musicians to the studio and got the recordings done. The music and songs were ready. Editing was finished too.

Now, what about sound? I went to a film school in Rohtak and met a student from the sound department. I asked him to take forty thousand rupees and clean up the sound. He said, "Maybe you're making a film for the first time?" I said, "Yes, it's my first feature film."

He smiled and replied, "It doesn't work like that.

- Dialogues are separate.
- Apart from that, all the actions in the film– the sound of footsteps, typing on a laptop, chewing food,

drinking tea, harvesting crops, the sound of the cycle, scooter, jeep, and hundreds of such sounds– are recorded as foley.

- Special sound effects are used in certain places.
- There is an ambience track, i.e., the sound of 'silence' at a location.
- The music track is separate.

All these tracks are then mixed."

Phew, it made my head spin. What a headache! I said, "But we have dialogues," and he replied, "No, even those aren't cleanly recorded. You'll have to do dubbing for that. Foley will need to be recorded at the studio. All this will cost a lot." This friend suggested, "Talk to the head of our sound department. Maybe they'll let you do it in college."

The idea was good. For college students, it would be a kind of internship– getting to work on a live project, having the experience of a feature film on their résumé even before graduation. I met with the head of the sound department, showed him the film. He liked it a lot and said he would arrange a screening as well. I requested, "Sir, please get the sound work done." He replied, "I'll need to talk to the Dean; I'll let you know." He kept me hanging for five to six weeks, called me to the college several times. Then he said, "You should get the permission yourself." Eventually, I spoke to the Dean one day. He said, "I have no objection if the head of the sound department agrees."

Now comes the twist. The very person I was relying on– the head of the sound department– suddenly backed out. He said, "The students' projects might get disturbed." I was very disappointed. So what to do now?

I searched on Google and found a studio in Delhi that had done dubbing for two films. After so many days, I called the film's actors again. We spent a month going to the studio, working one by one with different actors.

They had acted for the first time, so dubbing was quite a challenge. Matching the voice to the lips, delivering the dialogue exactly as it was spoken– it sounded difficult. But they understood and did a great job.

For sound editing, I connected with a graduate of the Satyajit Ray Film Institute who had worked as an assistant on a few films. I bought a 64-GB memory card, put all the dubbed dialogue tracks on it, and couriered it to Mumbai. It was a great offer for him– that he would be the chief sound editor of a feature film for the first time. On top of that, I was paying him. But he didn't take it seriously. He sat on it for three to four months.

While all this was happening, I wrote a Haryanvi song - 'Bhole Cutting Kara Le' (Bhole, get a haircut). In Haryana, most of the songs about Lord Shiva are such where he is associated with intoxicants like hemp and cannabis. I thought I should do something positive. A beautiful song of Shiva-Parvati, where there is a sweet bickering between them. This will present a beautiful form of love to the people. I directed the song, and also acted in it. I worked with some of Haryana's then-popular singers and a superhit female model. I spent fifty thousand rupees from my job savings. I thought the song would go viral, that it would boost my career. I gave the song to a hit Haryana company to release on their YouTube channel. The song got just over 425,000 views. I didn't earn even a single rupee in revenue.

Anyway, the female model told me that she acts in Ramleela every year and that the Ramleela director was looking for someone to play the role of Lakshman. I didn't expect to become famous from it. The money was only five thousand rupees, which was just enough to cover my bike's petrol expenses. But I did it because I had always wanted to play a role in Ramleela. This acting was very different from normal acting. Instead of subtle, realistic expressions, it required very expressionist acting. Your voice and body movements play a huge part. The director of the Ramleela auditioned me. He wasn't sure at first. He explained a few things, and after some days, he auditioned me again. He felt this time it was better.

There were 25 days of rehearsals. On the day of the performance, the director was worried about me. I was nervous too. There was a crowd of thousands in front of us. It started raining and the stage was wet. The first scene was in King Janak's court. As soon as I came off stage after the scene, the director gave me a tight hug. The audience applauded enthusiastically. Those ten days were amazing. When I would wait in the wings for my entry, people would come over just to meet me, showering me with praise. Someone said, "You and the person playing Ravan are the best; we come just to watch you." People would take selfies with me. Children would touch my feet.

But the most important thing was that same meditative feeling in acting. One day my family and a friend came to watch the Ramleela, on the day of the Lakshman–Sita dialogue. My friend told me that the people sitting in front of him started to cry. It was that same resonance all over again.

The sound work on '*Dararein*' still wasn't finished. At that time, short films were trending on YouTube. So I made an 8-minute short film - 'Take Care', an idea I'd had in mind for a while.

This 8 minute short film shows that when people migrate to other cities for corporate jobs, how old parents feel lonely in many cases. There is a popular saying about cinema - "Show, don't tell". The character in the film does not need to say - "Ah, I can't tell how happy I am today," rather his happiness is shown. Not only through the acting of the actor, rather the visual metaphors and the design of the image also imbue the audience with that feeling. I had not only the story in mind, but also the idea to make this film totally in this manner. Secondly, Bollywood loves melodrama; and a 'filmy' story means something different and strange, while on the contrary, I want to show ordinary life without any heavy drama. I think of showing all that we miss noticing in real life, in a way we have never seen. In this way, the film becomes a higher reality.

That's what I did in 'Take Care'. I made the film exactly the way I wanted to make it. It is a very simple film with only 3 scenes; hence very different from the usual films.

It was a two-day shoot. I hired two friends from Rohtak Film School for sound recording and mixing. This time, we did proper sync sound. I got the music from YouTube; I saw two videos in which Mozart's 'Turkish March' and Schubert's 'Serenade' were played by famous musicians. Obviously, Mozart and Schubert's music pieces are in the public domain, but permissions have to be taken for these recordings. I emailed them, saying I am making a short film; I want to use your music recording. I got replies from both places, that they had no objection.

It was my first time shooting on a DSLR camera, which I borrowed from a friend. I rented lenses from a camera rental. I did the writing, direction, camera, and editing myself.

Six Sigma films, a short film channel in Mumbai acquired the film. But the film had no familiar faces. There was no marketing push behind it. The film got stuck at only 14,000 views. Forget about any revenue. The film got nominated at a film festival in Lisbon, which felt nice.

I told the Mumbai sound editor - I want to send '*Dararein*' to the National Awards this year; finish the work quickly, it's been too long. To get the work done, I even went to

Mumbai. The work he had done was of sub-par level. I made the payment, but then I talked to sound editor who had worked on 'Take Care'. I made some payment and asked him to do something about it. He worked on it for days, and now the sound mix became a lot better.

A Marathi film produced by Priyanka Chopra had won four National Awards. I was also hoping that maybe we would win something for the songs. Or for the eldest sister-in-law's acting. Maybe even for direction. If nothing else, at least the 'Best Haryanvi Film' award.

Submitting a film to the National Film Awards is a struggle in itself. The film must have English subtitles. I did those myself. Then you have to be part of some Mumbai association. Register the film's title. Provide a copy of the script. Provide a translated copy in English. Submit the song lyrics. Trailer, teaser, posters - I made all of these too. There must be some screenshots of the film, and some working stills, like where the director is seen shooting a scene. We had never even thought of these things before. Especially since we had only one camera, where would we get working stills from? Somehow, we managed. On top of that, they asked for so many other things. An agent in Mumbai helped with this.

The biggest problem was that the film had to be submitted on Blu-ray and DVD. I called the government office and said, "Ma'am, Blu-ray was for better quality, but now we have 32 GB and 64 GB pen drives, which have more space than a 25 GB Blu-ray. So why not on a pen drive?"

But common sense and government rules don't fit in with each other. She said, "Just do what's in the rules." Finding a Blu-ray player itself was so difficult, and here we needed a Blu-ray burner. I searched on Google and finally found one. It took 30 hours to burn a single Blu-ray. This whole process cost thousands of rupees. Somehow, the submission happened, but we didn't win any awards. Neither for '*Dararein*' nor for 'Take Care'.

The idea of releasing on CD was no longer possible, because the CD circuit had shut down. Now, even Haryanvi content is being released directly on YouTube. My heart was filled with a dream to release the film in cinema halls. But that was a different matter altogether. You have to get a DCP made. Give 'virtual print fees' for the cinema hall in advance. If you're going to spend lakhs, you'll have to do proper marketing too; otherwise, what's the point? Even to release in just a few cinemas in Haryana, it would cost at least 80-90 lakh rupees.

What if I could find a release partner? Or an OTT platform? I took the film to NFDC's 'Film Bazaar'. It was a five-day program at a hotel in Goa. Made friends, took them to lunch, had conversations, but nothing materialized.

There, I met two government officials from Haryana, who had come for the Haryana Film Policy. I showed them the film. They were very impressed. They said, "This is the story of every household. It promotes Haryanvi culture. It gives a great message. Send it for the film policy.

Government grants are mainly for talented people like you, who don't have money. You'll get a grant, and the government will also get the film released."

Yet another hope, and with it, another struggle of submission. So many pen drives, so many script copies, so much paperwork. I made several trips from Delhi to Chandigarh. The screening committee meeting kept getting postponed.

Finally, one day, the director of that government department called. He said, "Come to Chandigarh quickly." The screening committee had watched the films that day. Some Bollywood actors and directors with roots in Haryana were part of the committee, as well as some people who had worked in Haryanvi cinema.

I reached there and introduced myself, "I am Vijeta Dahiya." One of the actors hugged me and said, "What a film you have made, man." A press conference was held. Even there, they said overall they were disappointed; the standard of films was low; but out of all the films they saw, only Vijeta Dahiya's '*Dararein*' stood out– a very emotional film.

There was another senior actress, who said that not only is the language of the film Haryanvi, but every aspect of it carries that fragrance. And she said she'd never seen such authentic performances, not even in any Bollywood film.

This praise from the screening committee members was published on the Haryana government's website, and it's still there. Yet even after that, I didn't get the film grant. Who got it, why they got it - let's leave that aside.

After that, I met with a Punjabi film company. Nothing worked out there either; as people say these days, if your film doesn't have romantic songs, big locations, or action scenes, then it's not cinema hall material.

So the point is, after so much effort, what I got everywhere was disappointment, disappointment, disappointment. '*Dararein*' was shelved. The lawyer who had played the role of the eldest brother suggested releasing it on our YouTube channel. I refused, saying, "You can't perform Bharatanatyam at a street junction. YouTube is a very volatile medium. People don't watch anything attentively, whereas our film demands full attention. We won't release it on YouTube."

So we started doing private screenings. We would rent projector screens. My wife felt that the film moved slower compared to other films; that the general public wouldn't like it. But every screening got a great response. In the dark, I would see people wiping tears from their eyes. For five minutes after the screening, a deep silence would linger; it was like a hangover of the film. Only after that would people start to discuss.

True that the film had not been released, but the film had been made. Although there were only a few people watching it without any ticket, yet the film was at least being watched. It was leaving an impact on people. The world would term it a failure, but in our eyes, we had succeeded. We had completed what we had started in our craziness. We had succeeded in making a film. No one could take that away from us. I had become a filmmaker.

Chapter -13

Stuck In the Maze

Now I wrote a short film of about 45 minutes - 'Opra' (The Other), where a married woman in a village is possessed by the spirit of a boy from a neighbouring village who was murdered 20 days ago. Has the boy returned to seek revenge? Or is the woman pretending in order to gain her freedom? Or does she have a mental illness?

I thought that if this short film featured a familiar face, it would do well and perhaps open up some opportunities. Through a friend of a friend of a friend, I managed to get the script into the hands of a Bollywood actress for the lead role. Her brother told me on her behalf that yes, the role is good, but now her brand value is too high; daily valuation running into lakhs; she can't work without payment.

Another Bollywood actress said that this story closely resembled her own life; something similar had happened to her. So in that case, she should definitely do the film? But no! She said that since it was personal for her, she couldn't do it.

Then I went to Amritsar to meet a senior actress from Punjabi cinema. We sat at a restaurant. I narrated the story to her. She was very polite. She said she would do the role, but I'd have to find the producer myself; I shouldn't expect her to get involved in that process.

Things were materializing on the film front. So I thought of writing. Where? I started writing on Hindi Quora. If I could build a following there, maybe I could use that to get a book published. Before I knew it, I had three and a half thousand followers - a decent number for a reading platform like Quora. I got millions of views. The comments were full of praise. People said my words gave them new perspectives on life; gave them courage. Quora awarded me the title of 'Best Writer' for 2021 and published my interview. After having written 274 articles in Hindi and 8 in English, I started to wonder, "How long am I going to keep doing this?" I got an invitation to the Quora Partner Payment program, but because the model seemed ridiculous to me, I couldn't bring myself to accept it. Instead of paying writers for writing answers, Quora paid people for asking questions. Later, this model became one of the reasons for Quora's decline.

One day, I just walked straight into a publisher's office. I met the publisher herself. I told her that I want to write, I want my book published; so please tell me what to write about. She said, "Come to us when you're so famous that we already know who you are." Ouch! Her words sounded harsh, but honestly, it was better than wasting my time with things like "email us" or "we'll let you know."

I went to another publisher's office. I said the same thing, and he asked, "Can you show me something you've written?" I said, 'Absolutely'. Someone asked a question on Quora: "Can you think of something strange?" I had written an answer to that. In fifteen minutes, I read it out to him. He said, "That's very well-written. Write a book to motivate young people." I said, "Okay."

I started writing the book. After a few months, I sent the publisher two books. The first was 250 pages long - 'The Buddha with a laptop' - and the second one also running into 250 pages - 'The Buddha with headphones'. The publisher said they'd publish the books, but I wouldn't get any money; that's just how sales work. I felt that if they themselves didn't trust their own sales network, then how could I hand over a gem to them?

Now, I started worrying about money. In the meantime, I had done a bit of work here and there. For instance, a senior from Ranbaxy started a company with a friend that acted as an agent between loan seekers and money-lending banks. One day, he asked me, "Vijeta, we have some branding work. Will you do it?"

I said, "Sir, I never did an MBA; I don't know a thing about branding." He said, "It's creative work, you'll bring your own vision to it. We need 12 infographics to run on Google Ads, and an animation video. We'll set you up with our graphic design editor; you just have to get it done from him. We also want your thoughts about our website. Tell me, how much money do you want?" I said, "Sir, it should be sixty thousand rupees, in my opinion."

He said, "Maybe you're not fully understanding the work; you'll have to come to our office and work for 10–15 days. It's hard work. Sixty thousand isn't enough; take one lakh twenty thousand."

Wow! Fantastic. Sir got me another job with a different company, too; they needed four one-minute videos for their product. I did that as well. But obviously, that wasn't enough.

Meanwhile, my parents also found out that I'd left my second job too. Actually, the son of a friend of my father's friend had cleared the SSC CGL and was posted at the Ministry of External Affairs. That uncle told him, "My friend's son, Vijeta, also works there; meet him, talk to him." He inquired at the office and learned that I had quit. He told that uncle; that uncle spilled the beans to my uncle; my uncle asked my brother; so now I had to accept it. It was clear to me that it wouldn't be long before my parents found out; so I decided it was better to tell them myself. I thought, "I'll tell them in the morning." That night was very tense.

Early in the morning, I wrote a letter and rode away on my motorcycle somewhere. My wife gave the letter to my parents. I'd already called my uncle and aunt to come by in the morning. My wife, brother, and sister-in-law were already there. Just then, another uncle, with a pretty progressive outlook, also happened to come over.

My father was surprised after reading the letter. Everyone explained to him, "If he had the confidence to quit his job, then he would surely do something wonderful; don't worry." My mother also said, "It's fine; he's always wanted to do something different." I got a call: "Where are you? Come back home."

Strangely, my father didn't make much of a dramatic scene that day either. When I got back, he was calm. Later, he even gave me money to buy a camera. Did I take the money? Absolutely. If your parents give you money without conditions, then there's no need to go filmy that I won't take a penny from anyone; They're your parents; their money is your money; just take it. So I bought a camera. Another foolish thing that I did.

You can rent a camera, and unless you have regular work for it, you really shouldn't buy one. There was no budget for making a new film. Finding clients for photography itself was quite a task. I wondered if I should start shooting weddings.

Once, I did shoot a wedding. Actually, a friend of mine had the same idea and needed my camera. He said his assistants would come to pick it up. I didn't want to hand my camera to anyone else, so I went along myself. His two assistants worked with me. For the first time, I saw a wedding from the photographer's perspective. I watched the whole wedding right through the wedding farewell. Staying up all night wasn't a problem for me. I enjoyed it. My friend gave me five thousand rupees. He himself had gotten only twenty thousand from the client.

I thought, if I do this, I'll need to set up a studio, get an office, have a website made, and hire three people to work with me. This was a full-fledged job in itself.

For a friend, I did a free bodybuilder photoshoot. From morning till evening, we did five looks in different locations and costumes. The photos turned out amazing. My friend was very happy. I thought, if I could do portfolio shoots like this, five looks for twenty-five thousand, I could make good money. It was a creative gig as well. I visited around 25–30 nearby gyms; talked to the trainers; showed them my friend's photos. I told the trainers to show these photos to their clients, give them my reference, and if a deal got made, then five thousand from the twenty-five thousand would be theirs. I even went to a protein powder shop and gave him the same offer. But finding clients willing to pay twenty-five thousand wasn't easy in my area. I probably should have tried in richer areas like Malviya Nagar or Greater Kailash. But that thought occurs to me now; back then, it didn't. If I'd done five looks for ten thousand in the beginning, that would've been fine, too. Anyway, maybe I just didn't have the conviction for this work. Maybe that's why I didn't try very hard.

I made two comedy videos for YouTube. 'Haryana Government Job Interview - Hardworking candidate vs Candidate with recommendation' and 'City Girlfriend vs Village Girlfriend.' Videos like these were trending on YouTube at that time. Both videos got five or six thousand views. But my brother once asked, "Do you really want to do this, or something more artistic?" I should have said that I'll make artistic films when I get the opportunity; for now, I'm making these because I can do so without a budget; even these have some acting, direction, scripting, creativity; what's the problem; there's no vulgarity; just decent comedy.

But I didn't say that. I can think of it now, and maybe it's good I can at least think of it now. But at that time, I didn't continue with it.

So, now the situation was:

- '*Dararein*' couldn't get released.
- 'Take Care' was stuck at only 14,000 views. I had thought that maybe Anurag Kashyap would happen to watch the film and call me to assist on his next project; but that didn't happen.
- The short film that I'd written - 'Opra' (The Other), I couldn't get a producer to back it.
- Quora didn't bring in any money.
- The book didn't get published.
- The Haryanvi song 'Bhole get a haircut' didn't lead to any offers, neither for lyrics nor direction.
- The photo shoot business hadn't taken off.

So, should I take up another job? Certainly not the kind of jobs I'd quit earlier.

One day, I dashed off an email to a famous Hindi journalist. His media organization's YouTube channel had over ten million subscribers then. In that email, I described my journey. In the end, the gist was that now I need a job. There was no resume, no cover letter in that email. Rather, it was a literary biography written in a storytelling style. It was, in itself, a work sample. I figured that he'd studied Hindi literature; he was an interesting person; so he'd at least read, perhaps reply to this odd letter.

He didn't disappoint. One day, his office called and invited me for a written test; they said I'd be perfect for their cinema section. They asked me to just check out their website. Oh, do they have a separate website as well? I didn't know. I checked the website. There was an article: "This director was told by Rajkumar - Even my dog wouldn't do a role in this film." If you google this, you'll find that article on just about every media portal - whether it's a sellout or honest media; every cinema desk runs film gossip like this. It's just that I didn't know this.

Whatever you search for on Google is what will keep showing up for you, and even if something is very popular but you've never shown any interest in it, then it won't appear for you. If you think about it, real life runs on a similar algorithm. You're more likely to interact with people who are like you. I never read film gossip, so that had never appeared in my feed.

Anyway, I thought it's not necessary that I'd get a gossip-writing job. There are also film reviews. Thinking this,

I went to their office. There was a three-hour written exam. One question was about Hindustani Bhau. But I had never watched Bigg Boss. I wasn't on Twitter. I wasn't on Instagram. I didn't see memes. So I didn't know who Hindustani Bhau was.

One question was to write about any one of the given five movies. Now, the problem was that I rarely watched films in the cinema hall. Cinema isn't time-pass for me. I've never really had such extra time in life. For me, a new film means any film I haven't watched yet, even if it's fifty years old. In childhood, I watched good movies on Doordarshan. Then I started watching world cinema on the UTV World Movies TV channel. When I had gone to the Satyajit Ray Film Institute for the workshop, the friends there loaded a lot of great films onto my hard drive.

That's why I had seen *'Garam Hawa'* (Scorching winds). I'd watched films by Ingmar Bergman, Wong Kar Wai, Satyajit Ray, Majid Majidi, Fellini, Martin Scorsese. But these movies that were on the exam paper? Of the five recent films, I'd only seen one - Saaho; that too, by chance, with a friend. I wrote about that. For the subjective questions, like describing my relationship with cinema, I wrote those answers fluently and comfortably.

The test ended, and just then that journalist came into the office. When he learned about me, he spoke excitedly - Ah, so you're Vijeta! What an amazing person you are, my friend. He praised my Haryanvi song profusely. He read some sections of my email aloud to the office staff. Then he said, “We’d love to hire you, but there’s a problem. It seems to me that you think you’re meant to do something great in life.”

I couldn’t say no. He said, “In our media company, there’s only regular work; I don’t know if you’ll like that.” I spoke my mind, saying that I wasn’t interested in film gossip, but I liked the other things they do, like film reviews, poetry, some shows - I liked all that. He didn’t like hearing that they do film gossip. He said, “No, we never publish gossip.” What could I say? I said nothing.

I got hired. The salary was 10-20% higher than what I earned at the Ministry of External Affairs. Then I started writing - “Whose sarees did Rohit Shetty used to iron?”

A friend asked about the new job; I felt awkward explaining what I now did. Still, I sent him an article. That friend, merciless as ever, said, “Will you actually do all this? There’s no fun in it; this isn’t work of your level.” Such friends are truly necessary. Anyway, then I wrote - “Katrina Kaif swept the floor at home during the lockdown,” “Salman Khan fed hay to his horse, ate some of it himself, video goes viral.”

To see some meaning in this work, I tried to add some value wherever possible. There was news that an actor from Aamir Khan’s film “PK” had died. So I took my time to find out exactly which role the actor played - the opening scene, where he’s selling tickets in black for a show; I added a screenshot of that scene. I searched for the actor's work on his Instagram. I found his showreel on YouTube; a scene from a play he had performed in. He had acted brilliantly. But imagine! He couldn't get work in Bollywood. He was under stress. Now he is gone, so I thought it was only right that people know about him; it would be a tribute to him. If ever there was something about Aamir Khan, I'd mention his film 'Earth-1947,' thinking that people should discover this excellent film.

I was told, "Why so much detail? Just do it quickly. You earn more salary than others, and you only do 4–5 articles a day? Set a target of ten articles." The logic was simple: more web pages, more views, more ads, more clicks, more company revenue. What could I do? I started writing faster.

One day, someone told me about the internal dashboard, where you could see the numbers on your articles. I looked, and saw that out of the month's top 10 articles, 6 were those written by me. Maybe my talent had a bit to do with it, but in my opinion, the main reason was that people read cinema gossip far more. Millions had read my articles. There were even YouTube videos made on some articles, and those views were separate.

Instead of feeling happy, my mind was shaken. On the dashboard, you could see the average time people spent on the page. I realized that, cumulatively, I had wasted millions of minutes. People could have done something better with that time. I felt like I was distributing opium to society.

I gave my notice to quit. I didn't have any other job lined up, I also needed the money, but I still felt like - leave it, man, never mind, I'll find something else. It was during the Covid pandemic; so we were working from home. My father would see me working until 10 or 11 at night. Even he said this time, "You need not work in a job like this; quit it."

For the journalist, it was a big shock - how could someone leave their organization, and that too, so soon? He said, "I can relieve you right away, but if you want, stay for a month's notice period and do what you hoped to do when you joined."

I said, "A few days ago, in the morning meeting, you said you wanted our media portal to be like Britannica, where there's information about every important thing: the French Revolution, the Russian Revolution, Indian culture; our portal should be a river of knowledge. So why not let me write a similar series? These days, words like 'left-wing' and 'right-wing' are thrown around randomly. If we talk about the history behind them, it would be beneficial for political discussion in the country." He said, "Okay."

I started writing. The first episode was about the French Revolution; he read it and liked it, and told me to continue. Then I wrote about Karl Marx's life. I explained his ideas in simple language. He liked that too. Then I came to the Russian Revolution. Now he asked me to get it checked by the assistant editor, who said, "It's well written, but it is scattered like sunlight."

What does that mean? What kind of simile is that? Is that praise or criticism? I asked, "If there's a problem with the structure, no worries; tell me, I'll fix it." He said, "Leave it; let go of this series." I felt sad.

For the last two weeks, I was asked to write general news. The journalist would say in morning meetings, "Why does everyone stay quiet; give some suggestions, or what's the point of the meeting?" The problem with me is that I take such things seriously and actually start giving suggestions. I asked, "Why do we publish so many murder and suicide stories?" The answer was obvious - readers take 'pleasure' in such news, and that's why those 'stories' do so well. It's like an open secret everyone knows but nobody says out loud. I said it, and made things awkward.

I was starting to realize that media organizations work like this. What is the breaking news; what's trending; what is today's big story that they'll spend all day writing news pieces about. The country's population is largely rural and agricultural, but their stories aren't 'exciting', and hence, hardly get any coverage. Sensational stories work great in the news business. But this is not something you say out loud. What you do say is that we're journalists; we're the fourth pillar of democracy; the country's issues are our top priority.

I saw that, unintentionally, I had put the journalist through a whole emotional ordeal. My only intention was to improve the quality of the media portal. Honestly, I liked him. Anyway, those last two weeks passed, and I took my leave.

Chapter -14

Flying In the Sky

One day, my wife said that Dhruv Rathee has posted on YouTube that he needs a researcher. I'd seen Dhruv's work since long ago. I liked it. I sent the links to my 8-10 Quora articles as a work sample. He asked me to write a test script about the Israel-Palestine conflict. I didn't know much about the topic. I wasn't an expert in geopolitics. People often criticize YouTubers, saying that they act as experts on geopolitics one day, fitness the next, then social issues. But the truth is, YouTubers or content writers are experts at just one thing: curiosity about different subjects, deep research, reading a lot, understanding things clearly, and then explaining them simply to people. I had become an expert in this work by now.

I started writing, and just kept on writing. Then I realized I'd written too much, so I made a short version. I added pictures in the document too. When I emailed both versions, the long and the short ones, I already knew I wouldn't hear a 'no.' Even though it was a bit late, there was a call a few weeks later. Dhruv praised the work: "You've written so wonderfully; let's get on to work."

Now, the amazing part is, Dhruv asked me to write a series, 'Basics with Dhruv Rathee,' in which we had to explain communism, socialism, and capitalism. Pretty much the same kind of series I was writing earlier. Dhruv also had the same idea in his mind that we should explain the meaning of these terms so that the range of political discussion can expand.

The first video on communism did really well. The editor was new too; he did amazing work. Then we did videos on socialism and capitalism. We took these terms out of New Delhi's seminar halls and made them reach the general public. Then we made videos about many great personalities - Raja Ram Mohan Roy, Rabindranath Tagore, Bhagat Singh, Swami Vivekananda, Dr. Ambedkar, and others. I also did voiceover in those videos; getting into their character, I recorded some of their quotes in my voice. In the comments, a few people even asked if it was the real voice of Bhagat Singh. Hahaha.

Then Dhruv said, let's start a series – Gems of India; can you go out somewhere and shoot something? Why not! I was yearning to shoot something. I took my camera, tripod, reflector, and reached Jaisalmer. There, I shot a documentary on Rajkumari Ratnavati School.

Then I shot a video shedding some spotlight on Haryana's Tree Man, Devendra Sura. He works in the Haryana Police, and on weekends, he works on planting oxygen gardens, i.e. hundreds of trees clustering together to make a mini-forest.

We did a video about Vikalp Foundation, which was started by software engineer Shankar with a few friends; these people either work in different jobs or study in college during the week, and on weekends, they participate in cleaning and beautification efforts.

Ravi Dahiya won a silver medal at the Olympics. I made a documentary depicting the struggles behind this victory. I enjoyed getting to shoot something after a long time.

Earlier, I used to charge two different rates for writing. For current affairs videos with a short shelf life, I charged less. To write videos with a longer shelf life, which could be watched even four years later, it required deeper research and more time to write. And hence, I charged more for those. Then gradually, every one of our videos took on this evergreen style. Even if the topic was current, the information we provided made it evergreen.

- For example, when we did the video about the old man's food stall *(Baba ka Dhaba)*, we thoroughly explained the concept of media trials in it.
- When Rahul Gandhi was disqualified because of a defamation case, we used the video to explain how defamation cases are used as political weapons across the world.
- During the Russia-Ukraine war, we exposed the global arms lobby in a video.
- When a comedian, cartoonist, or reporter was targeted, we discussed the topic of freedom of expression in detail.
- When we made two videos on Manipur violence, we not only talked about the present situation, but also dug to the root of the issue, gave historical background, and introduced the concept of neocolonialism.

We made videos on classist attitudes. We did a scathing critique of superstitions like astrology.

I have no hesitation in saying that each of our videos improved YouTube, added value to people's lives, and enhanced the national discourse on many issues. Journalists provide daily news, and of course, that has great importance in its own right. But keeping up with every piece of news every hour, releasing a video every day– that's not our cup of tea. Dhruv and I are unable to see ourselves as journalists. Dhruv likes to see himself as an educator, while I consider myself a thinker. That's why we both found this evergreen video style more appealing, and the audience liked this broader perspective as well. Hence, our video on any topic arrives late, but nonetheless, people wait for it.

I had thought, "let me do this work for the next 5–6 months, save up some money, and hopefully find a way into filmmaking." But eventually, I started enjoying it - both the work and Dhruv's company.

Here was someone for whom talking about Bhagat Singh wasn't just for the stage, rather we could talk about these ideas even in personal conversations; without fearing that the other person would mock this as being too idealistic or overly sentimental.

Instead of constantly ruminating on 'what will work', we could freely think about what we wanted to do, what was necessary for the country; only then would we think about how or when that content would perform well. That's why we even made three videos on such an offbeat topic like evolution, because we felt it was important for people to understand. With each video we were learning something new, and offering something new to the audience as well.

Some time later, '*Dararein*' got released. It became the first Haryanvi feature film to be released on MX Player. Still I didn't make money. After about 3 years, I only got around 7,200 rupees. But at the same time, Haryana's only OTT platform, Stage App, also released '*Dararein*'. They gave a decent amount– enough to cover the film's cost.

A few weeks later, I got a call from the Stage App team. They told me that '*Dararein*' turned out to be like that child who, with just a nudge, starts walking and running on his own. Even without much marketing from their side, the film was doing really well. They asked if I would like to make another film. I exclaimed, "why not!"

I quickly pitched them the concept for '*Opra,*' which I had already written. They liked it. I developed that screenplay further, adapting it for a web series. The budget for a short film in Bollywood is what you get for a feature film in Haryana. The experience I gained from '*Dararein*' helped here. I did the casting and finalized locations.

Whether it was camera, sound, accommodation or food for the crew, the costs were increasing on an daily basis. So, we made a shooting schedule of only 22 days. There was heavy fog on the very first day, so the schedule got disrupted right from the start. That's why we'd kept 3-4 buffer days in the middle, so that if anything went wrong, we could get back on track.

Apart from the fog, many other problems came up, but just like with the previous film, there was only one thing in mind: no matter what, the film must be completed. We used to return from the shoot by 8 in the night. I'd prepare for the next day's shoot until midnight, then wake up at 5 the next morning. It was so hectic that I lost four and a half kilos in 22 days. But still, I enjoyed it thoroughly. One day, I celebrated my birthday right there on set.

Later, the title '*Opra*' was changed to '*Opri Paraai*'. The web series was extremely well received by the audience. It became one of the most watched series on Stage App, and also won the 'Best Actress' and 'Best Web Series' awards at Haryana film festivals.

Even after this, instead of being a full-time filmmaker, I continued writing for YouTube. Not just for Dhruv, but also for other YouTubers. Including Dhruv, I've written for eleven YouTubers.

For example, once we went to a studio to record a song for 'Opri Paraai'. A few days later, the studio owner called. He said, "Brother, Fukra Insaan is here with me– talk to him." I thought, what rudeness – calling someone 'Fukra Insaan' (loafer guy) right to his face. Then the person took the phone and said, "I'm Fukra Insaan." I thought, how odd, he also calls himself that. He asked if I'd heard of him. I said, "Are you talking about the film 'Fukrey'?" He refused and then said, "I just did a video accepting a challenge from Mr Beast." At that time, I didn't even know who Mr Beast was.

I have overcome FOMO – Fear of Missing Out. People say, "Dude, you haven't watched Mirzapur? What are you talking about!" Then they would talk about the characters of Kaleen Bhaiya and Guddu among themselves, but still I don't feel like watching it. I haven't watched any of the Avengers movies. I don't let anything into my mind just because it's popular – whether it's films or YouTube, I look for what I actually want to watch.

So, even though 'Fukra Insaan' is popular, I had not heard of him. He asked me to work with him. I checked out his channel on YouTube, and could not understand what exactly I should do for him. I told him, "Abhishek, the kind of work you do is good; but I tend to do serious, meaningful content. I don't know why you think I could contribute to your channel." He replied, "No, you should. I now want to do something different myself."

So we did two videos. In one, Abhishek had to call a friend he hadn't spoken to for years. This reality-TV-style episode was actually based on real life. Abhishek was quite hesitant to make the call; but when I urged him, he did it. He became so emotional that he gave me a hug. He said it truly felt great– like a burden had been lifted off his shoulders; a long-lost friendship rekindled in a single day. His eyes had turned moist. When people watched the episode, they got emotional too. Many commented that after watching it, they also called their old friends.

Then we did another video that I mentioned earlier about – with the farmers, where we helped them out of poverty:

- Gifted a wheat-grinding mill to a farmer so he could mill wheat and sell directly to customers.

- opened a small eatery for a family right in their house courtyard, and
- helped a dairy farmer.

Once, I got a message from a Quora follower saying - "Brother, my friend works with a motivational YouTuber; I told them about you, they'd like to talk to you." And that's how I connected with Shakeel from the Coolmitra channel. We created an astounding video on communication skills. We did several other motivational videos as well.

I wrote about mental health for one YouTuber, about fitness for another.

All this was increasing my own knowledge and benefitting my personal life as well -

- For example, I always had this question in my mind: "Which came first, the chicken or the egg?" I did an episode on this with Dhruv and finally got the answer.
- While writing the 'communication skills' video, I learned that we should match the other person's energy and speed. I tried it, and found that indeed it made conversations smoother.
- I wrote a video about fitness. Though I've exercised since childhood, I wasn't accustomed to doing strength training. After researching and writing the video, I understood its importance, and began doing strength training along with cardio and stretching.

Working with so many different YouTubers kept the job varied. Also, I was getting unique insights from each of them.

But the question remained: when I'd already released one feature film and one web series, why hadn't I started full-time filmmaking, as I'd planned earlier?

I even got an offer for a third film, which I mentioned earlier. He is a very famous comedy YouTuber from Haryana. He watched Opri Paraai, loved it, and called me. I went to meet him. He told me about a crime-thriller story, but it didn't fit my bill.

Likewise, once the content head of Stage App called. He said, "Vijeta ji, I've written a story; why don't you make a short film on it." The story was about a boy who goes out to party with his friends in the evening; in the dark, they accidentally hit a biker and run away; the next day, he finds out that it was his own brother whom he hit and who died. The story was okay, but just okay. So I declined this offer as well.

People always say, "Never let opportunities go; the right opportunities don't come often, seize them." But my habit has always been to let go. Quitting jobs, refusing admission to the Film Institute after getting selected, rejecting these film offers.

People say, "You are letting go of a golden opportunity to become a YouTuber; you are marvellous at writing; you have no hesitation in speaking in front of the camera; imagine how much money you can earn by becoming a YouTuber." In multiple podcasts, people have asked why I don't start my own channel. I say, there is no difference between me and Dhruv; I see this channel also as mine; here I'm able to share my thoughts; I like to write, and that's what I'm doing.

Actually the world has bestowed upon me a certain responsibility, which I have to fulfill. You see, very few people seem to be free in this world. Children are crushed under the pressure of studies. When they grow up, they get trapped in the web of unemployment. Those who do get jobs, become slaves to their bosses. They're stuck in toxic work cultures. Their boss is a slave to his own boss. The top boss is a slave to the owner. The owner fears the politicians; he's forced to make political donations, or else he would face a raid.

The politician is under pressure to win elections; he is under pressure to maintain his public image; he can't really say anything out of the blue that most people might disagree with. On top of that, he's bothered by journalists and YouTubers who criticize him and say, "Stop your dirty quid pro quo with the crony capitalists."

The richest businessman is also a slave to his own greed; he just can't find peace anywhere. The artist is a slave to the desire for fame. He can't think beyond 'what will sell'. And even if he thinks of something, the producer doesn't let him. Listen to any actor, singer, or director's interview and you'll often hear the same thing - they can't work on what they actually want to.

If you ask anyone, "Are you truly happy?", people get unsettled. If you probe more, they might even get offended. Films constantly remind us that if life is poison, then you have to drink it. Poets say, "Why should a man be rid of sorrow before he dies?" Philosophers say there's no such thing as free will; they say society has conditioned you. Writers say that a man is just a puppet of his circumstances.

Amid all this, I worry that maybe the very concept of freedom might become blurred in the world. That maybe people will start to believe that living in joy is just impossible. That's why I carry the responsibility of remaining free. To hell with success, to hell with career. If I don't feel like doing something, I simply don't. I am a living, breathing Statue of Liberty. I even call myself an independent filmmaker.

Besides the two film offers I rejected, there's still a third ongoing offer - to make gangster and crime films. The people at the 'Chaupal' app said the same thing. '*Dararein*' was released there too, and during the discussions they told me the same. I narrated three stories: one was 'Monu Rockstar,' the second was about farmers, the third about exam paper leaks. But even there, the content head said, "We want a gangster film."

Once again, I felt there's no hurry to make a third film; let me keep writing all the same.

The book that I had written earlier and which couldn't get published then - 'The Buddha with a laptop' and 'The Buddha with headphones' - one of its chapters was released as an ebook, 'Power of Universe.' You can read it at the Dhruv Rathee Academy. More ebooks will come out in that Life Series.

During the last Lok Sabha elections, Dhruv and I created several masterpieces together. Deep down, Dhruv and I always doubt how much real impact our videos have, if anything at all. But when we meet people and they say, "During the last elections, you guys shook the government," it makes it seem like maybe we did something after all. Below every video, there are thousands of comments praising it. Someone messages to say, "You have saved democracy in our country." Someone else says, "You are the Bhagat Singh of our times." You shouldn't let praise carry you away, but I'll admit that hearing those things does feel good.

But it's not just about what others say; you also get a sense of satisfaction yourself. When you're doing your best work, you feel joy right then. You feel like - Wow, I wrote something amazing today; that was satisfying. Like the way we discussed meditation, resonance, and joy - I won't feel these things while making gangster films.

It's not that I've given up the idea of making films. I'm still trying. A few months ago, I went to Mumbai. Someone invited me to the premiere of a film. There, I met Rajkumar Hirani. I mentioned that I work with Dhruv Rathee. He greeted me warmly. No, he didn't offer to produce a film for me, but who knows, maybe someday that'll happen too.

Someone suggested that I should first release 'Monu Rockstar' as a novel. I liked the idea. So I'll work on that. Then there's my story 'Hansdev,' which I thought of as a film. In this, people start disappearing from a village, and rumors are that a 300-year-old saint, Hansdev, is behind it. Sub-Inspector Sumit Sehrawat is investigating the case. Maybe this also would work well as a novel.

For now, there's enough money in the account. Not crores, but enough for me. So I'm thinking about doing some theatre again. Maybe not in Delhi this time, but in Rohtak. There's also a Haryanvi YouTuber who makes comedy videos. I saw he follows me on Instagram, so we talked. He suggested I come over and that we make short films and web series for his YouTube channel. Maybe I'll do something with him.

Dhruv and I are also discussing a reality show that would change the very direction of Indian politics.

So there is a lot on my platter. Let's see what works out and when. Am I still struggling? Yes, and maybe I always will. Because I don't want to be settled, going to an office from 9 to 5 every day, doing the same thing. I like doing different things, so I have to keep seeking out new things. Someone else might call it a struggle, but for me, it's more like an adventure.

When I look back, I feel amazed at all that I've done in my life -

- Written more than 100 poems, some of which you might have seen on Dhruv's Instagram;
- Written many YouTube videos;
- Many stories which are on my blog;
- Six songs– three for my own films, and three more separately;
- 280 articles on Quora;
- 'Power of Universe,' now an ebook, after this 'Control Your Destiny';
- Acted in plays;

- Made 2–3 comedy videos on YouTube;
- Doing some creative things on Instagram these days; sometimes it's my poetry, a new thought, a story, or some short act;
- Wrote, made, and edited two short films;
- Wrote, directed, acted, and danced in a Haryanvi song;
- Made a feature film;
- Made a web series; (did writing, direction, editing, and even acted in them)
- Shot documentary series;
- Played a role in Ramleela;
- Did social work projects;
- Travelled in India and abroad;

My family is happy; I party with friends, and often meet fascinating new people. Ah! Life is beautiful. Even after doing so much, there's still a sense of freshness. It feels like the game has just begun.

❑❑

Chapter -15

Step Into the Arena

The great poet Zauq said, "Life brought us here, so we came; when death takes us away, we will go. We neither came by our own will, nor will we leave by our own will."

But we can choose to live on our own terms. At the very least, we should try. Look up and see how vast this world is; there is so much to do here, yet you have tied yourself to one post. Sitting in a corner, you are merely watching the game of the world, but the real question is: when will you step onto the field yourself?

Again, I say, if you don't have a passion, it's not your fault. The way schools and colleges are, it's difficult to have any passion for anything. Explore.

We've already talked all about this. The first requirement will be to change your mental frame. You'll have to break free from the prison where everyone is running a race. Just moving from one jail to another isn't smart. You have to move toward freedom.

You must have heard about the tragic demise of Anna Sebastian, who worked at an associate firm of Ernst & Young. That's when we did a video on toxic work culture. Anna's mother wrote an emotional letter to one of the company's bosses, which we shared with you. That was when I felt the urge to write this ebook. I realized it was necessary. So if your job is severely affecting your physical or mental health, you should surely quit. If you have life, you have the world.

But if you can manage for a few days, don't quit suddenly out of frustration or in a wave of excitement. If your mind is set on the path to freedom, then explore on weekends. Break out of the rat race. Explore while temporarily leaving behind the thought of money. Try something that sounds fun, that adds value to the world. Go deep into that work. Learn the skills. Take up freelance work, or do an internship with someone. If you don't feel passion for that work, try something else.

One day, you will definitely find something that gives you deep joy. From that, an urge will arise inside you– now this is what I must do. You'll feel it every day, like a burning desire. At that point, there is no more doubt. Walking that path becomes the only choice. Then, prepare your blueprint.

We discussed this as well– the middle class has some surplus left over, which can serve as initial capital for a business. Besides that, various models like venture capital, self-help groups, cooperative models, and micro-finance are breaking down the wall between capital and labour. Just like I used my job salary to produce my first feature film, *Dararein*, by myself.

Somewhere, a mother and son started a pickle business with ₹4,000 and gradually grew it to earning two and a half lakh per month. Somewhere in a village in Bihar, a woman and her husband's sister started their own business with their own money, went to Shark Tank, didn't get funding at first, but received it later. On Shark Tank, I saw another business– FarmDidi– which three people started after leaving their corporate jobs. Today, thousands of women are connected to their venture.

So it's no longer about capitalism versus communism. The point is this: if capitalism exists, opportunities should exist for everyone. The point is that more businesses mean a more decentralized economy. Employment can be arranged for all. Everyone should be able to enjoy their work.

This business, FarmDidi, even prints the names of the women who made the pickle on its packets. Imagine how beautiful that is.

That's one part– raising capital. The second change is in the means of production. In Karl Marx's time, businesses belonged to the capitalist, and he alone owned the means of production. Even fifty years ago, starting a business meant buying machines, owning land, and setting up a factory. That's why business used to be such a heavy word.

But today, the scenario is very different.

The first factor is the service sector, which didn't exist back then in this form. In 2021, 67% of global GDP came from the service sector. For example: servicing and repair of electrical appliances like TVs, radios, refrigerators, and ACs; computer repair; electricians; plumbers; tuition teachers; gym trainers; wedding planners; party planners; party chefs; birthday-party magicians; interior designers; wedding choreographers; tourist guides; bird-walk guides who explain birds in sanctuaries; trekking guides– and so on.

For these, you don't need any means of production. You just need to be an expert in a particular skill, and people need to have your phone number. You can distribute flyers through newspapers, hand out your visiting cards, register for free on Google Business, or create an Instagram handle.

The scope of these services keeps expanding. There's an expert who is very good at speaking and making jokes. People invite him to their weddings to interact with guests, entertain them with jokes, make everyone dance, and conduct games - all to add a lively touch to the party. He earns 40-50 thousand rupees for one night at a wedding. These are called wedding hosts, wedding MCs, or wedding anchors.

There's another service I mentioned earlier: people take others on village tours, and they have a page on Instagram. Many people, rather than seeing village life as a showcase, want an authentic experience.

Party chefs don't have to worry about how they will sell their food; they provide only their cooking services. People call them to their homes or the party venue; all the raw materials are there; the gas burner and cookware are there; the chef comes with an assistant, and they prepare the food for the guests.

The second factor is that today, the means of production/ services can be rented. In my village, a boy was teaching boxing at a sports academy. Forty to fifty kids started learning boxing. The revenue was split equally between the academy owner and the boxing trainer. One day, the academy owner got greedy and said he'd take 70% and leave 30% for the trainer. The boxing trainer rented his own place; all the kids followed him, and now he was getting the entire 100%.

People run coaching centers on rented premises. They rent a shop, fill it with salon equipment, and start running a salon. Someone has rented a shop for mobile repair services. Not just that, people are even running entire hotels on rent. It may surprise you, but it's true.

I have a friend who is an excellent singer and musician. He lives in Goa. There, his wife has taken three or four large houses on lease. The owners of these houses are occupied elsewhere with their own work, so they prefer a steady income from rent. My friend's wife leased and beautifully decorated these properties; she has a great understanding of hospitality. She takes bookings online, and tourists come to stay in these properties. For housekeeping, room service, and cooking, she has employed local people.

In many places, resorts are also leased out this way. If you have managerial skills and business sense, you can run such a business.

Now there are even models where you don't need to rent any property, office, or shop at all. Once, near our house, someone started a business called "Mr Idli" right from their home. They hired two people for delivery. There was only one item: four idlis with chutney. Flyers were distributed in newspapers. That's how everyone got their number. Many people run tiffin services in this manner.

These days, you don't need your own resources, even for marketing and sales.

For example:

- You can sell your product via Amazon, Flipkart or Meesho
- If you're in the food business, customers can discover you on Zomato and Swiggy; this way, you can run a cloud kitchen from your home
- Taxi drivers register on taxi apps like Rapido, Ola, or Uber
- People offering tourist accommodation list their properties on Airbnb and get bookings through it
- Party chefs register themselves on ChefKart, COOX, Take a Chef, Cook and Chef, and Zomocook
- Party singers can create their profile on The Live Show or Book My Artist India

These are called aggregator business models.

Many people make their products and supply them to retail outlets; they simply enjoy making the product. Conversely, some people outsource the manufacturing part: for example, they buy plain white T-shirts in bulk and only do the printing. They enjoy designing which image or quote should go on the T-shirt.

You can do this too. For example, if you're not interested in farming, then you could buy from farmers and sell it further; that way, you are handling just the marketing and sales. By removing so many people from the supply chain, you are the only link between the farmer and the customer. The farmer's income increases, the customer gets products at a lower price, and you can earn as well.

Or, as in the example we saw earlier: in the village, someone has a house, they know how to cook, and you just look after the demand side of this village tourism business. Again, you don't have to buy any means of production here.

You don't even need a business website now, because even if you have one, search engine optimization is a big challenge in itself. So, people now make an Instagram page for their business, which works as a homepage. You can run ads from there and get new customers. The digital world has changed business a lot.

This brings us to the third factor - the digital economy of the digital age. Not only offline businesses can be run more conveniently, but many jobs are entirely digital. You already have a phone and you can start uploading Instagram reels instantly. If you want to upload YouTube videos and need editing, free editing software is also available. For background music in videos, there's YouTube Audio Library; you can also pick an audio track on Instagram. For content, you can use AI.

A few days ago, a 17-year-old boy messaged me requesting mentorship. He works as a waiter in a hotel. He shoots and edits videos on his phone and uploads informative short videos on YouTube and Instagram. It felt good to see this.

You already know that you can earn from YouTube AdSense and that brand deals bring in money. So, in this business, the 'means of production' is the platform, available to everyone. Nowadays, people are also earning money from Twitter.

Some people provide news updates through Twitter, while others are YouTube journalists. Hearing this word, perhaps the name of someone like Ravish Kumar comes to your mind, but I want to draw your attention to those local journalists who are raising issues of their villages and towns through YouTube. Mukesh Chandrakar's village, Basaguda, was affected by Maoist violence, which forced his family to relocate. He lost his father when he was very young. His mother raised him and his brother Yukesh while working at an 'anganwadi'.

When Mukesh turned 22, his mother passed away from cancer. Mukesh made ends meet by selling local liquor, mahua, and at other times working as a bike mechanic. His brother Yukesh became a freelance journalist, which sparked Mukesh's interest as well. He started doing ground reports for Sahara, News18, and NDTV, going deep into the forests of Naxal-affected areas to report. The cameras of these news factories visit his area occasionally only to cover Naxal encounters. That's why ground reporters like him do not have permanent jobs with news channels; their income isn't stable; they often live in poverty. Mukesh refused to become a cog in these news factories.

He started his own YouTube channel - Bastar Junction, where he highlighted all those issues of the tribal communities that he wanted to; matters related to water, forests, and land. He showed villagers' protests, reported on fake encounters, revealed the poor condition of health centers, and showcased how Naxals destroy public property. Pressures came both from Naxalites and the government. But he was immensely popular among the tribals. In four years, he posted 486 videos; the channel gained more than 150,000 subscribers. Mukesh started earning ₹20,000 a month, and in one month, he even earned ₹50,000. Now, he had some stable income. Then, one day, he exposed corruption in a major road project and was murdered. Don't focus on the fact that he was murdered; it's not that if you become a YouTube journalist, then you also will also be killed. Notice instead the *samvega* he had; he truly loved his work. That's why he took the risks involved. He was able to create his own news institution. He could report news from his own region. Maybe hardly anyone in that area knows about YouTube's 'Super Thanks' option, yet he was able to earn a decent living from his channel.

Local journalists like him have always been, and always will be, extremely important for democracy. Because, by voting, you don't choose a king who then does whatever he wants for the next five years. You need to keep an eye on your MP, MLA, or village head to ensure that they do not engage in corruption and that they work for the people. You have to check whether teachers in government schools are teaching properly, whether government hospitals have medicines, and whether electricity and water facilities exist for people. You have to ask why there are potholes in the roads, why so many thefts are happening in the area these days, and why is there a lack of employment opportunities for the youth? Journalists keep an eye everywhere on behalf of the people; they report; they ask the government the people's questions. Creating a ruckus in the name of debate in a big news channel studio is not journalism. Real journalism is what reporters like Mukesh do.

Local news should get the most space in newspapers because it affects us the most. Ideally, people should buy their local newspapers and financially support them, or support the local journalist's YouTube channel by making payments through UPI. Local brands should be able to advertise on those YouTube channels. This model is working. Whether in Uttar Pradesh or Maharashtra, in many states such local YouTube journalists are emerging, and are getting financial support from the public. There is no need for a journalism course to become a true journalist. You don't need a big building either. No need to buy a TV or radio channel. YouTube and Instagram have given you the 'means of production/service.'

Even coaching centers that prepare students for government exams have now come to YouTube. Teachers like Khan Sir are teaching thousands of students live on YouTube. Even poor students are able to benefit from this coaching.

Besides being social media influencers, YouTube journalists, and YouTube teachers, many people are now doing digital marketing as well. Someone manages influencers. Others have strong networking skills, allowing them to connect influencers and brands and launch their own agencies. None of these require any special means of production.

Recently I met a friend who is a YouTuber uploading content on science topics. He revealed to me his new plan that since he now has a know-how of YouTube, he is going to build an ecosystem for influencers spreading scientific temperament in society. He would help them with all aspects, from catchy thumbnails to brand deals with smaller brands. Thus, there would be hundreds of others like him who would join him in the mammoth task of spreading rationality across the entire country. This is the *samvega* rising inside of him.

There are options like web designing, graphic design, video editing, film editing, and color grading. For these, you might need a powerful desktop, but advanced software like DaVinci Resolve can be installed for free. Or you can use software like Premiere Pro on a monthly rental basis. Many podcasters and YouTubers rent studios. Camera, mic, and lights - everything is available on rent.

When it comes to acquiring a skill in the first place, there's plenty to learn for free on YouTube - photography, filmmaking, food recipes, dance, music, acting, business tips, learning English, digital marketing, and much more; you'll find top-notch masterclasses.

Dhruv offers a course on becoming a YouTuber. Imagine learning from one of the country's most successful YouTubers. The relationship between offline and online courses is like that between theatre and cinema: an actor may have to do 500 shows of a theatrical play, but a movie can be watched in 500 places at once. That's why online courses are cheaper than offline ones. If Dhruv teaches 50 people offline in a five-star hotel conference room, maybe he will charge two lakh rupees per person for a five-day workshop. But when it comes to online courses, you can get the course for 3-4 thousand rupees. You can watch the course as many times as you like; you can pause or rewind anytime.

For just 500-600 rupees, you can get a 90-day editing course. Earlier, you had to go to another city for an editing course, and the fees were very high. Now, you can learn editing from home.

Even with offline courses, many short-term options are now available. Start learning and practising.

Then start working alongside your job. If your job has strict rules that say you can't do any other paid work, then do it for free. Prepare your 8–10 work samples.

You can even do internships without getting paid. It's a great way to learn and gain experience. Many people would gladly accept an intern available for free. Don't think that you're working for free; rather, think that you're learning for free. Who knows, they might even give you a stipend out of appreciation.

An internship usually makes us think of a company, but actually you can intern anywhere– even at your local Aggarwal Sweets or a bakery. See where the raw ingredients for bread and biscuits come from, watch the process of making biscuits, observe the packaging, and help manage the sales counter.

In a company job or internship, you might not get to explore as much as you can while interning at a local bakery; there's much to observe and learn. This is not a new idea. Every bakery has interns; the only difference is that those interns are poor. Middle-class people want jobs at biscuit companies because jobs have prestige. Rich people don't need to learn as interns; they just start a business. But if you go for such an internship, nobody is going to stop you.

You can volunteer at an NGO on weekends. You can intern with a wedding choreographer. Try an internship at a boutique and see how to deal with customers, how new customers are acquired, where fabrics are bought from, and how much margin is left– learn everything. You can intern with a Zumba trainer. The benefit is that starting something new won't feel so overwhelming then.

The heaviest burden is people's expectations. Since you left the rat race and chose a different path, your decision has become a question mark in their lives. That's why all eyes are on you. It's running in their minds– "let's see what he will be able to do." Not everyone is like this, of course. Some people may be genuine well-wishers who will encourage you. But many others would be just waiting for your decision to fail. They're ready to say, "See, I told you it doesn't work like that." This fear creeps in: what will people say if I fail?

So, when you work on fixing your mental framework, you also need to set your ego aside when you step out of that rat race. That is the real path to freedom. People say, "Your success is the best revenge; shut your critics up with your achievements." Don't get caught up in such nonsense. You don't have to prove anything to anyone. You wish to live your life in peace; you want joy in your life– that's it.

Another problem is that sometimes even well-wishers pile up so many expectations on you. It's not their personal thinking, but a societal pattern. Someone is earning ₹70,000 doing a toxic job. Another person is also earning ₹70,000 happily doing the work they love– isn't that better? As per common sense, if the money is the same but you have much more mental peace, then that's better.

But no, according to society, if you quit your job to start something new, you should be running a million-dollar business. Your startup should take over all of India. That is what they want from you.

There's a person earning a lakh per month while cribbing about his boring job. Someone else, also earning around a lakh per month, is doing small roles in TV serials or films. Isn't that person better off, earning the same money doing what he enjoys? But no, people will say, "Bro, when do we get to see you on the big screen?" They'll expect you to be the next Shah Rukh Khan. Whether it's Bollywood or

Hollywood, you should be everywhere and win the Best Actor Oscar.

If it's stand-up comedy, you'll be compared to Anubhav Singh Bassi or Abhishek Upmanyu. People will ask how soon you'll be that famous. If you become a YouTuber, everyone will demand that you get the YouTube Golden Button.

But why not ask them: in the company you work at, when will you become the CEO? Ask a government employee if he'll become the Cabinet Secretary. No, right? So then, why force this basket of senseless expectations on other people's heads?

Leave it, don't say anything. But remember, these things are nonsense. You've already set out on an adventure; you're breathing in the open; you're enjoying your work.

Another quirk of a capitalist society is that there's no limit to expansion; keep expanding as much as you can. But why? Do you really need to design clothes for all of India? Leave some things for others, too. Why should everyone want to be Bernard Arnault? If your single shop brings in ₹4–5 lakh per month, why open a second branch? Spend the rest of your time with your family, meet friends, travel, work out, read books, and watch films. So don't cave in to pressure from critics, or well-wishers, or yourself. Whatever you do, do it in a relaxed manner.

So that's it. Here's everything summarized briefly:

1. Quitting your job isn't some kind of fashion trend. If your job doesn't alienate you from your true self,

the work pressure isn't overwhelming, the hours are reasonable, you have time for yourself, you like your work, and you enjoy it, then stay in your job. Although such people are unlikely to be reading this book, if out of curiosity someone picked it up and got this far, don't get needlessly swayed. If you're happy, that's great. Continue your job. If you're not happy with your company, see if there's another place where you might find happiness. All the things discussed–manageable workload, time for personal life, enjoyable work, joy in the work– can you find these elsewhere?

2. If you've decided that you can't enjoy any job, then the question is: what now? If you don't have a passion yet, then explore. How you spend your weekends will determine your entire week. Use your weekends to see the world.

   By now, you probably know whether you're a science person or have some artistic creativity. Are you an introvert or an extrovert? Do you prefer research or operations? Do you prefer working alone and focusing on minute details, or do you like managing things with a team? You can take a personality test if you want. Consult a career counselor. Or even ask AI for suggestions: "I'm this kind of person; what career options might suit me?" Whatever fields come up– five, ten, twenty– start exploring them. One month, two months, three months, however long it takes.

   Go to watch theatre on weekends, read books, attend music concerts, join a film club that holds screenings;

watch world cinema you've never seen, go to the circus, watch a magic show, visit a painting gallery, attend a photo exhibition, try a bird walk, join a photography workshop, go to a seminar hall to listen to a lecture on the economy, attend a journalist's book launch– these events are open to everyone.

If an ethnographer or psychologist needs to conduct a survey, help them with fieldwork; DM someone from an advertising agency or a logo designer on Instagram and start a conversation; if someone's making a short film, help out on the set; visiting a big company is hard, but you can visit the premises of a small business. If someone asks why you came, say you're a journalist, a YouTuber, a sociology student, or a documentary maker; you could make up anything.

Go to the village fields, help with the harvest, bathe in the tube-well pool.

Learn something new; if something seems a little interesting, dive in. The more you dive in, the stronger your interest will grow. One thing or another will become your passion.

3. Learn that thing properly– through YouTube, online courses, a workshop running on five or six weekends, or a more extensive offline course– whatever learning method is convenient for you.

Will you take a job in this new field, freelance, or start your own business? This would depend on the work. Suppose you like statistics; maybe you'll want a job in an analytics firm. If you enjoy video editing, freelancing might be better. If you're interested in organic farming, that could be a business.

4. Now start working on this new thing on your weekends. If you can get some freelance work, great. If you can find an internship, even better.

Otherwise, you can start on your own. For example,

- Create concept notes and storyboards for ads for 10 different companies. A friend of mine even made free ad videos for a cafe, saloon and a priest. He is now using these work samples to pitch to other small businesses
- Design logos for some imaginary companies
- Download videos of someone like Dr. Vikas Divyakirti giving a speech, and edit them with great visuals; make 7-8 reels
- Write five songs
- Design some clothes

If you need to apply for a job or freelance gig, you can definitely attach them as work samples in your email.

If you want to start your own business, upload these to your business's Instagram page. For instance, if you tailored a suit, make a ten-second video showing the tailoring process and the finished suit, and upload it. That's a place where people can see your work. At the end of the reel, you can say, "DM to get such designer suits made."

If you're a makeup artist, upload 5-6 videos showing different makeup styles. If you're a portrait photographer, post 5-6 portraits you've shot. The people whose photos you've taken can tag you as a collaborator on their post. If you're into village tourism, first take some friends there, and have them post reels tagging your business page.

5. Pay off your loans; adopt a minimalist lifestyle with low maintenance and therefore low expenses. You have to get your mental framework right throughout the entire process.

6. Once you've done all this and the work starts coming in steadily, you can hire someone and pay them a part of your current salary. Then, after a while, you could leave your job. Or, if you'd rather handle things yourself, you might quit your job right at the beginning itself and go all-in on your new work.

By moving step by step like this, you can accomplish the biggest of tasks. It isn't hard. Don't be afraid. You can definitely do it, and you should. You have only one life, and you deserve to enjoy it.

❏❏

So our journey together stops here. How did you like the book? You can send me your feedback on Instagram. My Instagram handle is @vijetadahiya1. I hope this book will help you on your path to fulfilling your dreams. See you again with another new discussion.